ELIZABETH REEDER

Elizabeth Reeder is originally from Chicago and lives in Scotland. Her stories and experimental essays are widely published and broadcast. Her first novel, *Ramshackle*, was shortlisted for a number of awards including a Saltire Literary Award. She's a MacDowell Fellow and a senior lecturer in Creative Writing at the University of Glasgow.

ALSO BY ELIZABETH REEDER

FICTION

Fremont (Kohl Publishing, 2012)
Ramshackle (Freight Books, 2012)

An Archive of Happiness

ELIZABETH REEDER

Penned in the Margins

LONDON

PUBLISHED BY PENNED IN THE MARGINS
Toynbee Studios, 28 Commercial Street, London E1 6AB
www.pennedinthemargins.co.uk

First published in 2020

Printed and bound by CPI Group (UK) Ltd, Croydon CR0 4YY

ISBN
978-1-908058-77-5

*This book is dedicated to ARTT who has
my heart, every minute, day, year, decade.*

*Every archive reveals the questions held by
the archivist as they gather and sort knowledge.
This means the archivist exists as a fugitive element
within the archive.*

F. SKIRVING

But she did look back, and I love her for that,
because it was so human.

K. VONNEGUT

An Archive of Happiness

THE AVENS FAMILY TREE

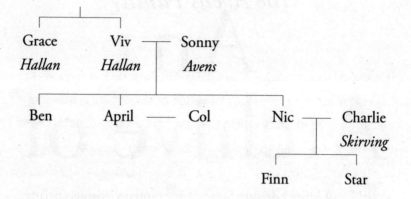

Grace *Hallan* — Viv *Hallan* — Sonny *Avens*

Ben — April — Col — Nic — Charlie *Skirving*

Finn — Star

CHAPTER I

The Avens Family

It was mid-afternoon on a Thursday, the summer solstice, and the branch of the granny pine at the edge of Grace's garden had been precarious for months and creaked a bit in the increasing wind. Beneath the tree, April and her dad, Sonny, were slapping the yearly coat of paint onto the fence. It wasn't going well. The paint was old and lumpy despite Sonny's attempted vigorous stirring.

He swore under his breath, cursing his sister-in-law. 'Buying a new tin of paint wouldn't have killed her.'

April noted his frustration when something wasn't done as he'd do it, which would be just as half-arsed, but in a different way: he'd have bought new paint but he'd have forgotten to clean the brushes before putting them away the year before. Little flares of dread at the coming days rose in her. Nothing specific but something; just tiny accumulated disagreements and resentments they'd all have to navigate. 'The paint is perfectly fine. Put more of your back into it and the lumps will go.'

'You spent too long living with her.'

April had lived with her Aunt Grace for a number of years when she'd dropped out of university, and she didn't know where she'd be if she hadn't. Since March she'd been living in a cottage that sat on the southeast side of the same hill as Grace's house, which was to the northeast. Her dad, newly arrived this spring, got the cool, stable light of the north. Her twin sister, Nic, lived two hours away on the northwest coast and her brother, Ben, would be out to sea anywhere his work took him. Their mother was a broken satellite circling and they never knew when she might plummet unannounced back to Earth.

April thought of the individuals in her family as they moved through the world, each in their own place but connected in time, and sometimes when tempers or resentments or impatience flared she imagined them all meeting at the stone ruins of the abandoned crofts that sat on the top of the hill she, Grace and her dad shared. All six adults arriving, backs to each other like in a Western and someone would say, *Ready. Aim. Fire.* When she imagined this, she knew the guns held blanks or paint balls or those wee darts with cushioned tips. Although, as their history showed, they were not adverse to using their fists, they weren't the kind of family to fire real guns at each other; not really, not even in this escapist flight of fancy—though sometimes, wouldn't it be easier if. April turned back to the paint and her dad. 'I stirred it last year and it was easy.'

He handed her the tin with a genuine humph. She half-heartedly ran the stick through the paint a few times in a figure of eight motion and it all came together. Sonny pretended he hadn't been watching ready to make a jibe if she failed, but instead picked up the brushes and handed one to her. The paint sat between them as they dipped their brushes in turn and applied a thin protective coat to the fence.

April sang under her breath. Sonny watched the weather come in.

'My mum used to creosote not only our fence, but the whole house.'

He'd grown up on the Black Isle, thirty miles or so away. His parents were both immigrants who met here—him from Egypt, her from Spain—and they'd disapproved of his marriage, of her mum. He never talked about his parents and since he'd brought them up, April said nothing to draw attention to that fact. 'Did she like getting high on the fumes?' She fake-staggered to make her point.

He considered this. 'She applied it every few years, like clockwork, letting no one else help her.' He paused. 'Yes. Yes, I think she did.' He laughed and April imagined his mum leaning in closer to the freshly sealed surface, giggling. Happy. Taking it where she could get it.

A gust shoved her dad's arm away from the fence and his trousers were slashed with white. The tree groaned but held firm and a shadow fell over the yard as the sun abandoned them.

They barely had time to gather everything together as a mid-afternoon summer storm rushed in with lightning and a few sure gusts: the usual when heat builds and needs to be dispersed. It signalled the start of the Avens family reunion.

The family didn't do other holidays but tried to get together every summer for at least a few days because that's what families are supposed to do at least once a year. There were good memories of late-night loch swimming, exuberant games of blackjack, as well as the dramatic consequences of this many people attempting to share a small space: the swing incident, the award-winning breakup of Grace and Annie, hundreds of micro-aggressions and tensions, the bull in the yard and the red-rag April held up to it. And then there was the incident with the axe.

They were angry and funny and exposed and there was a mother-sized absence in the middle of their family and if they poked it, it growled. This was how they were and with this many Avenses together almost anything could happen. Add in another moody element, Mother Nature, and this was what you got: a wind so strong it could knock you off your feet. Daughter and father made their way to the house. April opened the door and Grace lifted her head. Both women smiled.

'A sailor I know says there's always weather on the solstices and the equinox. They allow space for it, and don't make any big travel plans.' Grace looked at the rapidly darkening sky.

'A sailor you know,' April said as she held the door open with her hip to let her dad through and made the outline of womanly curves with her hands. The temperature dropped and the colour of the day became a sort of otherworldly greyish purple and the rain pelted down. 'And plus, what does "there's always weather" mean? Of course there's always weather.'

'Bad weather, Patience.' Grace's nickname for her niece who had so little and yet tried her aunt's so much. 'Don't give me your attitude.' Grace certainly didn't miss April's moodiness around the place. But then she watched her with her dark hair and how she'd settled into her body in recent months, and she realised she did, she missed her cheek.

'After every storm, there's an uplicht,' April said, perhaps quoting a ballad or tune learned from the band she'd been playing with, occasionally, the Scots newer to her tongue, but suiting her.

'Sometimes quicker than others.' They all looked north where, past the broody clouds, a patch of blue could be seen.

Sonny stepped past Grace who was in the kitchen, in her

element, cooking the day's feast, and crossed the room heading for the shower room in the corner. Ben, Sonny's eldest, now thirty-one, with his black eye and recently freed-up schedule (i.e. he'd been fired that morning), was in the shower as the storm hit.

Sonny knocked on the door. 'Ben.'

'Aye, Dad. I hear you.' His shout was an acknowledgement and held only a faint tinge of resentment.

And then a flash, boom and shudder. A branch of the gnarly pine slammed down onto Grace's fence, giving itself a lick of fresh paint along its bark. As it landed it gouged out a bit of her garden and tickled the decking that edged the back of the house. They looked towards the burst of movement and noise and noted the new space in the canopy opened towards the sky, with luckily no damage done to the house. The fallen branch was the size of a small tree and yet not even a needle had touched the house proper. A coven of three granny pines watched over Grace's house and so this branch could be considered a gift (and locally sourced firewood), but now the fence needed mending so the crofter's cows could be kept out of the garden.

The abstract threat of lightning was one thing, that very real crash quite another, and that was it for Ben's shower. It'd been cool and long enough to get the brackish loch water out of his hair and from behind his ears, although he did stay in a minute longer to let his heart calm, just a bit, for his worry about the coming days and weeks outweighed his anticipation of the evening or any sense he might be needed to help clean up a mess.

Off went the water. He only had to survive until Nic arrived and distracted them all from themselves. Nic lived eighty miles away, as the crow flies, and would be driving down with her husband and their three-month-old baby, Star—such a brilliant name—in the backseat. They'd pick up Finn from nursery and would then be heading down here. Ben was looking forward not only to a deflection from the colourful array of bruises his face displayed, but also to Nic's way—an art—of putting the family at ease. Her kids would help too, the inquisitive toddling boy and the excitable newborn who would need to be held. Her husband Charlie was good for a laugh or for some clumsy action that would break through any Avens-created atmosphere. Nic's company was always an invitation to stay a bit longer and be yourself. Ben glanced at his watch: ninety minutes, he guessed; she'd arrive and the whole world, the world of the Avens family, would become better.

He heard his aunt say, 'Tomorrow Victor the bull will be in the field,' as she started to assign tasks that would require tools.

When exiting Grace's shower, you had to have all your bits covered, and Ben made a fully clothed entrance into the living room, having gone in prepared with boxers, jeans and a T-shirt. By the time he emerged, his dad was standing there with goggles and gloves and the promise of the chainsaw waiting for him outside once the storm passed through. Ben shook his head.

'Have April do it. She's the man you're looking for to do that butch stuff.'

'Don't talk about your sister like that.'

'I don't mind,' said April, already eyeing the branch in a mercenary way.

'She doesn't mind.' Ben grinned at her and raised a hand in greeting. 'Hey bro!'

She bent her arm at the elbow and exposed her biceps, which were, honestly, only average on a body that did nothing to flaunt or hide its basic femininity. Her muscles were unimpressive but her will was mammoth and that got her through. Ben was well toned and proficient enough with a chainsaw but with April around, why bother? He was functioning on very little sleep where as she, who was also functioning on little sleep, was actually bright-eyed and energetic, full of the flush of new love. He remembered when Nic had just met Charlie, she'd been exactly the same—full of the heat of it, the possibility. Ben had known that feeling when he met Sonia, but it hadn't lasted. Sonia had been vocal about how he was making mistakes, pretending to be a type of man he wasn't, and that he could change that. She'd said she liked this other Ben better. Ben shook off the frustration and sadness that memories of Sonia caused in him. He had hopes for April and Col.

When Ben said April could do it, Sonny looked at his son with disappointment, perhaps, for the briefest second, like he could resist what his family had become. It passed, defeated, dramatic, like the lightning burst, and he smiled and turned. 'April, I have the perfect job for you.'

As he turned, for a minute, both father and son were aligned, squared shoulders, dark wet hair (one from the shower, one from swimming and the storm), a beautiful soft sort of sorrow and joy in their demeanour, as if they were the space between an inhale and an exhale. Sonny took one and then another step forward, his arms outstretched with an offering towards his daughter.

Ben looked to Grace who approached him, having missed his arrival, and she gently touched his face and the plaster on his brow before pulling him into an embrace, and he let her.

'When will your fighting be over?' She whispered. Both of them were thinking about the punch-up between his mum and him, all those years ago, which hadn't been his first fight, but the one with the greatest consequences, and the one he couldn't shake himself free from.

His body didn't feel peace or resolution but he let himself be held. This was a home of sorts, Ben knew. Grace's hug bound him here, grounded him just as everything had started to flutter, as if she knew he was planning either an escape or an ambush, thinking those his only two choices, given everything.

Outside in the garden, April and Sonny were heading towards the fallen branch at this, the start of the Avens family reunion.

About a mile away, heading for Grace's house, was Col, whom April had invited and told to arrive anytime. Col drove carefully through the squall, thinking that the water table could use the rain, and aware of a clutch of flowers on the passenger seat, two bottles of fizz (the real stuff), a few steaks for a grill (a guess at the set-up for the celebration), and such a pounding of the heart it was an effort to keep a relaxed grip on the steering wheel. April Avens. Now there was a woman you could settle down with.

Earlier, Nic had tried to snatch a power nap while Charlie packed everything into the car. She knew she should be sleeping because she was bone-tired and could feel a headache coming on, but instead she was listening to him singing to the baby.

April and Ben had been spending more time with the kids this spring and had started to mimic Charlie. Singing out of tune they'd say: 'This is your papa.' Singing in tune they say: 'This is not your papa.'

The off-key rendition was an ugly sort of beautiful and it's what put the kids to sleep. If that wasn't an argument for nurture, Nic wasn't sure what was.

Once she heard Charlie say after singing *really* out of tune: 'This is your mama'. Singing slightly more in tune: 'This is not your mama'.

And so she was kept humble. His singing grew quieter and she knew that Star had fallen asleep and so too did Nic, briefly, thickly.

Charlie had been up most of the night with Star, hadn't slept or napped, and so when they were finally ready it was quarter past four and Nic slid behind the wheel. It was her favourite drive, down along these quiet roads, the torque pressing on one side and then another as she took the curves.

All day on the summer solstice there's a sense of darkness being banished. Of the world being outlined with light, even if faint in the early hours. In other years there had been fog so thick she couldn't see the end of the car when driving. A real pea-souper. And then it felt like winter and all possibility of forty-eight hours of sunlit clarity gone. This year though, packing up the car, the bright blue sky promised a midnight swim. Star's first. Finn might paddle and Charlie might have to take him back to Grace's, or maybe April or Ben or Grace would do it. And they'd float there. Dad would join them, yes, and April would carry Finn to her own cottage later. She'd promised Finn that he could sleep within the trees. She'd promised a fire too and roasted marshmallows, but if he was tired that could wait until tomorrow. And plus, in this heat. The field trip to the Summer Isles was going well and they'd pick Finn up on their way down. Finn's teacher had texted all the parents to say it'd been a good day and that they'd be back at the harbour by 4:40. *Try to be sharpish*, she said. *They're wired and tired and looking forward to seeing all of you.*

Just off the collection of potholes they called their croft road and onto the main road the view out to the sea loch opened up and the water reflected the deep curved blue of the sky. Nic started to know it now, what the feeling was, that had been approaching all day. Anticipation in her chest, behind her eyes. April's exuberance, the brilliance of Ben's coaxed smile, Grace's food and drink, offered so freely. Her dad's awkward belligerence about rules and roles and yet, in his flawed way, she knew he loved them all.

Her whole family would be at Grace's. Ben had texted her this morning that he'd been fired—unceremoniously put on the first helicopter off the rig—and so would be there too. Ben's difficulties were clearly coming to a head with this morning's punch-up. She was looking forward to seeing him, to helping him stay off the rigs, to start to talk about the things he held hostage in that tight chest of his. She thought about her mother briefly, trouble-maker and problematic absence, and a familiar worry agitated a tender, fluttering spot on her jaw.

The road unwound before them and the rest of the world flickered at the edges of her sight. The blue of the air expanded and swooped around her and her hands turned bright like they were suns; her heart and belly too. A light powered through her, had been building all day and was, for that instant, only pleasure.

Well, maybe. As the blue scooped her up and gravity pulled her down, she knew its edge had shimmering questions.

At Grace's, Sonny was in the garden again, and Grace painted the fence April and Col had mended, in a fashion that was quick but good enough for now. The rest could wait until tomorrow or the day after. A solid breeze kept the midges close to the ground and only Sonny got bitten because he was on his knees deadheading flowers in the still spot by the house Grace had assigned him. She was too much of a sweet meal for them, apparently.

Ben was cleaning the grill for the steaks that would be slapped onto it later. He remembered the last time his mum had been with them here, sixteen years ago, and how they'd avoided each other, but she still gave him instructions on how to do almost everything. The love, the anger, the impatience. They weren't talking because he'd been kicked out of another school, and she'd had to be that sort of mother, again. They'd not been getting on but he found, deep down, especially when he noticed her red eyes and the balled tissue in her hand, that he felt for her too, but this sympathy somehow only gave breath to his resentment. Today, watching his dad and Grace work, he touched the butterfly bandage on his brow and felt the light pain radiating out from his fingertip, and he wondered what his mum might be doing now.

April and Col had disappeared off for a walk in the woods. 'We'll not see them again,' Sonny said.

But Grace wasn't so sure. 'Sometimes a quickie is enough, a sort of tantalising snack.'

'Stop it,' Ben said. 'Both of you. I don't want to think about April shagging. Or you either, Grace.'

'Okay.' She capitulated although she'd gotten them all thinking about young love and snatched intimacies. 'I do think they'll be back. Col seemed curious about us. Like someone who is entertained by family dynamics. He might even be looking for a family.'

'This family?' Ben asked.

'Why not? We're as good as any.'

Ben and Sonny laughed at her joke.

'Well, better than some, anyway.'

Pointing to some rocky soil that was overgrown with chickweed, Sonny said, 'Didn't you used to have something here? Little purple flowers.'

Grace stood up and glanced to Ben, hoping Sonny would take the hint and stop this line of questioning.

'Yes, Suzie had wild thyme planted there.' The house had been Suzie's before it had been Grace's.

'Ah, I remember now. Viv used to love wild thyme,' Sonny

said. Ben stiffened and so did Grace, who shot Sonny a hard look but he was oblivious, which is how he'd survived in this family. The sound of metal on metal as Ben cleaned the grill increased and finally got through Sonny's thick skull. He turned to Grace grappling to change the subject. 'What happened to *your* thyme?'

She nodded. 'I had some work done to a patch of damp at that wall and it killed it. A shame, really.' She did wish that she'd done more to protect it too. The scraping eased and Ben was listening. 'Especially now that it's overrun with weeds. Although,' she drew out a bit of a smile in her voice, 'did you know you can eat chickweed? Full of good stuff, supposedly.'

'If you feed us that, none of us will ever come back,' Ben said, looking up and smiling.

'Got it. I'll just sneak courgette or beetroot into the chocolate cake like I did when you kids were little.'

'You did what?' Ben laughed, thinking of all the delicious things he'd eaten that Grace made. None of them had felt like one of his five-a-day.

'Ach, we adults need to amuse ourselves in small ways when it comes to kids.' And they all went back to their small tasks, re-balanced.

A little while later, Grace noticed two roe deer edge the woods, their heads low in the long June grass. A tortoiseshell butterfly landed on a sea pink beside her, its wings wide open, and it put her in mind of the small metal music box she'd come across the other day at the back of the old dresser in the living room, which she hadn't wound yet but, if memory served, it had been recorded on a day like today but when the kids were young; a keen worm aerated the soil and Sonny moved his shovel so to avoid it and heard the two-part call of a redstart and was thinking about re-planting the thyme on the sly; Ben found that, for no reason at all, he could not catch his breath.

The car smoothed around the curve. The young couple from the croft heading out to Achiltibuie. Nic drove. Her hair, which Helen had always thought of as black, looked auburn in today's bright sun. She slowed a little in front of the house, waved and shouted, 'Hi Helen!' as she flew past. Music blasted from the car and her husband waved and then turned to his wife, singing too. Helen saw the infant car seat on the seat behind her, and a baby, born a few months ago. A girl named Star. She didn't know about these parents and these names. Finn, whom she looked after occasionally, must be at nursery. The summer afternoon was beautiful, and later she'd garden, keep herself moving or she'd stiffen up. Just beyond her house the road took a sharpish curve and the car raced towards it. Nic was a local and knew these roads so well, but a ripple of concern moved from Helen's belly to her ears and instead of turning towards the house she paused and listened.

CHAPTER 2

April loved a good ceilidh. Here in the stone village hall, with all its side doors open to the half-light, as the clocks approached midnight and would soon fall into this summer's solstice day, locals and incomers danced and were, maybe, almost, too drunk. At any moment it could tip over into an over-enthusiastic reel or, rarely, into a non-committal fist fight.

She noted the sureness of Col's hand in hers as they stood and chatted to Siobhan, her Aunt Grace's next-door neighbour. Siobhan's eyes shone when she talked with them and April knew how they looked. Perhaps some thought with all the flirting they'd been doing that they should get a room rather than displaying their desire on the dance floor, and she had plans for later in her small cottage and its big-enough bed.

They danced the Gay Gordons, the band making a brilliant ruckus, stretching the stamina of all but the fittest of the participants. When it ended, small pains bound the dancers together—hips, knees, lungs—and people sat at the weak-legged tables and quenched their thirst with a cheap ale from the tap or a simple dram served in a tiny plastic cup (or irreverently swigged from a hip flask), and yet they looked to Mairead, the fiddler and singer for the band, to make the next call to the floor.

'All out on the floor for a Strip-the-Willow.' She stretched out her arm, her fiddle with the bow crossing the strings held casually in one hand. Some callers were neutral, all business, but not Mairead who believed that each session made a new family of us all. 'Many of you will know how it's done but our own April Avens and her partner…'

'Col.'

'April and Col will lead us off. Now everyone get yourselves back onto the floor for the final dance.'

April pressed Col's hand lightly against the outside of her thigh, as in a pact.

'We've got this,' April said to Mairead as she and Col took their place. Even at this late hour, even for this wildest of dances, people congregated into jostling lines. Some dancers prided themselves on the bruises they might leave on the arms of their partners. Some partners could handle it and matched the pressure, the tension, the speed of the turn; some gave as good as they got. Men had brawn; women elbows and heels.

As this haphazard congregation danced, this thigh flashed and another, a woman's skirt twirled up, as might a man's kilt. It was an equalising dance floor. April grinned, nodding to people as together she and Col reeled down the centre aisle, their fellow dancers opening up for them. She moved away and came back, hooking into Col's arm as they birled— away and back, all the way down the line. When they got to the end, they stood with one leg stomping to mark time, clapping clapping, and cheering other pairs as they took their turn. April caught Col's eye, threw her head back and her arms open, and whooped.

Ceilidh dancing isn't about intimacy and romance, it's about working yourself up into a right good sweaty lather. It's a wind-roughed forest. Your feet, unabashed and proud, connecting to and stretching away from the heather-bound soil, blood pumping through your trunk, and the branches and leaves are the communal flail, the shared throwing open of arms as if roused by gales.

April looked around at this mid-summer's dance as young and old and ugly and beautiful all danced together, thinking, who isn't really quite beautiful in the midst of a dance? The room had been stripped of the impact of awkwardness because it was everywhere and handled with humour and grace and generosity. It is assumed you will mis-step, that you might elbow someone by accident (and apologise on the next pass).

We build something here, April thought. It lived for hours and days in blood and breath and on skin, and if you were lucky enough to go home with someone and get naked; if you were lucky enough to have a first kiss or a first shag after a Ceilidh, you'd know it was really something. April knew it would be something.

Standing by their cars, April and Col kissed. The clock on the dash blinked from 11:59pm to 12:00 to 12:01am. Col dropped the car keys into April's open palm and she drove Col's car along the narrow roads like the local she was, with Col's hand on her thigh. A maddening and steadying touch. She parked at the bottom of the hill.

'Don't you have a drive up to the house?'

'Nope.'

Holding hands they walked side by side through the woods. Col said nothing; April said nothing. The play of light, the crunch of fallen branches breaking again beneath their feet, so faint. They knew something about each other: how to push at their bodies and how to show restraint, tenderness.

A snipe drumming made the air substantial. Hearts beat out of their cages. Through the trees, with heather and blaeberries beneath their feet and bracken brushing their legs, they came to her tiny cottage. They did another turn on the porch, a makeshift, tight twirl. They were both good movers, fast and then slower and even closer. Her hand moved down Col's back and waist, and ran it along hot skin and down, beneath and between fabric and bands. A ripple, a pressure, a rush. A question. There could have been panic but there wasn't.

'Oh,' April said, still close, closer if that's possible. 'Well, this will be interesting.'

A quarter of a mile to the northeast, around the waist of this hill, Grace dreamt of baking a rich chocolate cake. The rim of bowl was the exact circumference as if she'd stretched out her arms to hug a bear. In fact, that's how the bowl appeared in the dream. She conjured it by making a circle with her arms and bringing the tips of her fingers together. Voilà. She put it on the counter of the kitchen island and held aloft her left hand, palm up, and into it arrived a wooden spoon, which she brandished like a conductor's wand. Each wished-for ingredient appeared on the kitchen counter, as if by magic.

Another quarter of a mile towards magnetic north, also around this hill, Sonny was awake when he wanted to be asleep. Viv's email, received just before he went to bed, had unnerved him.

He'd tried to sleep but he'd fallen into the memory of her the night before she left.

They'd been naked in bed with the sweat of sex drying and Sonny had a leg flung out of the covers, an arm too. His other arm was pinned between Viv's legs. Viv clamped it there, perhaps in a bid to shore them against the threatening break up that was not fierce but quiet and more looming because of it. They had never, even in the midst of the fiercest argument (and there had been many of these), or the coldest night, slept with nightclothes on. Nakedness encouraged friskiness; intimacy encouraged honesty. It had been a theory they'd practised, despite ample evidence to the contrary. They'd always fought, but it changed. Their bitterness infecting everything; her growing rage impacting how she looked after their kids. He kept mentioning it, warning her about it. In this naked state the words took shape again before he could stop them. 'You should take it easy on Ben.'

Viv unclamped his hand, pushing it and him firmly away to his side of the bed and pressing the sheets between them to make a fabric wall. 'He goads me and has no respect.'

'Earn it.'

'Don't put this on me. He needs a role model and all he has is you, the one who drags us all over the world with your morally questionable work.'

'I would like to see *you* support this family.'

That's how this argument always ended. She'd become pregnant before finishing uni and he'd encouraged them to go away. He had a lead on a job with a civil contractor to the military that had let them leave Scotland and travel. 'I'll make good money,' he'd told her, withholding what he suspected might be involved, and they all knew how that'd turned out.

The day after this disagreement there was an exchange between Viv and Ben. His usual explosive strop; her misguided attempt to earn his respect; her threat to send him away to school. There was blood. There were ultimatums. There was departure.

And today, sixteen years later, for no reason Sonny could fathom, he'd heard from Viv. He'd had occasional emails to say she was still alive, but this one held a simple question: *Are you all at Grace's, like usual?* Boom. Just like her to seek out the nuclear option. Just like her to rob him of his sleep.

Across a breath of land and an exhale of the North Sea, Ben Avens's hand curled into a fist. The sky was still aglow on this midsummer night and his breath caught at the beauty of the light and the ghostly grey-blue sea and the powerful construction of the rig.

As he landed a brilliant punch upon the cheek of his colleague everything grew brighter and clearer and he knew this was his last day ever on the rigs.

Seventy-two highland-road miles away by car—quicker as the hooded crow might fly—the Avens-Skirving family was asleep. This was a very temporary state.

CHAPTER 3

Swing

One year, the year Nic and April were six, on a little patch of public ground down from Grace's cottage, Sonny built a swing set and they named it a playground. You could just about do that sort of thing if you didn't tell anyone your plans and/or seek permission the council wouldn't give you. Sonny spent five days of their family holiday welding together a simple structure that would hold two swings. He worked intensely from morning to night and didn't like to be disturbed.

Grace helped him to erect it in the middle of the night. It was compact and all metal—metal legs and crossbar, metal chains to suspend the swings and only the seats of the metal swings were covered in thick rubber attached by big metal bolts.

Some of the neighbours whose houses also hugged the road complained about the illegality of it; others brought their kids along, and the swing set settled into the landscape quickly enough. The adults could see the playground from Grace's kitchen and could hear their twins' discussions and arguments. Ben was only ten but had deemed himself too old for such things and played football with friends he'd made or they'd go skinny-dipping in Belter's Loch, a quick ten-minute dash up the path over the hillside. He spent nearly every waking minute in the water and he always came back nettle-stung and gorse-scratched and paid little heed as Grace stuck out Savlon in his direction. Sometimes they'd find a crushed fistful of leaves in the pocket of his shorts and figured that someone at some time had shown him nature's remedy. Neither Sonny nor Viv could guess what it might be and Ben informed them in a dull, dry response,

'That's dock, guys, it's good for the stings.'

As the twins swung on the swings, they aligned in time and arc with each other only occasionally, only by accident. The girls looked nothing like each other. Or rather, they looked like half-sisters with different fathers. When Nic and April stood back to back they were the same height. Nic had deep red hair and April had black hair. Curly. Straight. Nic was good with people and numbers and her hands; April was sporty and irascible, and good with people too, but in a different way. They had exactly the same smile, which transformed their serious-at-rest faces, and as they played together each day they changed and changed again.

All day the twins were out there swinging and the adults prepared one meal or another, drinking tea, lemonade and beer, doing a bit of gardening and upkeep around the house to help Grace out. Her old stone cottage wasn't impressive but it also wasn't ramshackle. Built in 1834, it was doing just fine. It was charming and basic and furnished with indistinct, inherited furniture—what was left after the rest had been culled from the house by Grace after her stepmother Suzie's death, to make room for paying guests.

Talking, drinking and working alongside them each summer there was always a different woman acting like she was part of the family. She'd talk too loudly, but usually pitched in with every task and would make Grace laugh as Sonny sssshh'd his grumpy judgmental resistance.

Sonny knew there might be many polite ways to discuss Grace's life choices but that wasn't how the family talked about it back then, which was, mostly, not at all. What they knew was that Grace traveled all over the world as a private chef for this famous person or that millionaire and never settled in one place and then, during their summer visits, Grace would introduce them to these women. A different one each year. Viv never asked, neither did Sonny, and Grace never said anything except, 'This is Melody' or 'This is Rose.'

'Such pretty names,' Viv and Sonny and their polite kids would say.

'It's as if she only dates daughters of hippies,' Viv finally said one summer's day when the girls were still toddlers, and it was out in the open. Sonny said nothing: it was one thing to think it, another to say it out loud. He knew, he absolutely knew he should say something to acknowledge this obvious truth that had been spoken. Grace went out with women. Grace shagged women. But he knew he should not voice what he wanted to which was, *Is it safe for us to leave our kids with her, if she's a, if she's that way inclined?* This was wrong thinking, he knew, and not really how he thought of it now, but those were the only words that would be leaving his lips back then and they were unacceptable. He'd think on it, work through it in all its implications, and come back to the subject with something useful and insightful. He'd bring it up, which would show his ease and his courage to be so manly in the face of his quickening invisibility.

So that night, instead of saying anything, he reached out and ran his finger over his wife's hip bone and then down between her legs.

'So many of them are so pretty,' Viv said and she turned to him, pulling off her nightshirt over her head, tossing it on the floor. Sonny knew that now was a good time to say absolutely nothing.

Over the next year, he wasn't polite or quiet when he

thought about it or, sometimes, he thought about raising it when they were living abroad and conversation was slow, where telling a story with a bit of edge could come in handy, could bring a bit of social power and maybe business favours later on. So far he'd held back, maybe because he understood what it was like to be different, but if he did have the gumption to tell the story at some point he'd raise it as Grace herself would. He was sure of it.

What she might say was that, speaking of herself in the third person: Grace Hallan is gay. She's happy, joyful, crazily free and carries life lightly. She might do stupid things, which a future generation of kids will come to say is 'so gay.' And she likes women. Always has.

Year after year, Grace introduced them to one beautiful woman after another: Cherry, and then, Paris, and to this year's Joy.

They didn't complain because there was something they could all appreciate about these beautiful women, and they were summers of loving. Grace and her girlfriend upstairs, Sonny and Viv on a bed made of cushions downstairs, in the middle of the sitting room floor, with their kids safely out in their tents reading surreptitiously with head torches and spending time in much more innocent worlds beneath the covers.

At dawn, in the year of the swings, before breakfast, the girls were down at the playground again. If they hadn't been twins egging each other on at every step, Sonny wondered if they'd ever learn to do anything at all. If one did something the other would do it better. And at six years old, April always appeared to do better. She moved more confidently, but Sonny was never quite convinced. The whole time Nic was learning, and it would stick deeper in her. She was banking every titbit of knowledge—figuring out angles and momentum and force, so it didn't surprise Sonny when he heard nothing for hours and then a scream, from Nic. He shouted for Viv, but she was nowhere to be found, and so he ran because although his girls shouted all the time, they didn't scream. Nic had fallen to her knees in the grass beside her sister who was out cold, bleeding profusely from the head. Sonny couldn't see the wound at first, only that April's whole face was blood and flesh. And then he saw it, a swing-shaped point of impact on her forehead, bloody and already swelling. Missing her eye by an inch, if that.

'I'm sorry, I'm sorry, I'm sorry,' Nic repeated.

Sonny didn't ask. He gathered April into his arms, carried her to the car and laid her out on the back seat, while Nic climbed illegally into the front and buckled herself in. Both daughters were quiet and one of them guilty. At the A&E at Raigmore they pulled the curtains round, strapped April down and gave her only a local, which Sonny knew was a mistake, and sure enough she woke up and screamed and screamed and screamed.

Sonny held April's hand and Nic clung to his leg and put her hand into his coat pocket looking for safety. Instead she found his car keys and grasped the ring as if she'd found a place where she hadn't just rammed a metal swing into her sister's head. April calmed down when they'd finished stitching her up: five stitches, a proud Frankenstein scar across her forehead, which would be easily enough hidden by hair, if that's what she chose to do. The straps across her chin ensured she'd kept her head still, even as she screamed. Sonny didn't turn away but he had wanted to. Not from the blood or the injury but from the fact that he couldn't be the one to put her back together again.

Afterwards, both girls got lollipops.

April was asleep before they even got her into bed; Grace had given hers up for the wee'uns.

'The swing moved so fast,' Nic said.

'It's metal,' Sonny said, feeling the pads of his fingers in the palms of his hands, remembering smoothing the ends, trying to make them curved enough not to cut small fingers. He'd never thought about other impacts they might have.

'I thought she'd move out of the way. She didn't move.'

'Maybe she didn't see it coming.'

'She sees everything coming.'

As April recuperated up at the house, Grace pampered her with homemade soup and her favourite biscuits, gingersnaps, and Sonny watched Nic down at the playground, let that swing arc from side to side all the next day. She'd let it go, watch its trajectory, catch it. Push it in a harder, faster arc, catch it. Every variation you could imagine and she knew, she knew.

Her dad came to get her for dinner because her mum had gone into the hills with a tent. 'This is my holiday, my time off. You deal with it,' she'd said when she'd left.

Her dad hadn't called her in for dinner, but walked down to get Nic and stood beside her as she let go of and caught the swing. He watched too, calculating, fascinated. After a while, they made their way to Grace's and didn't say anything. Her heart flew about in her chest and she didn't know if it was joy or worry, pleasure or guilt.

Nic watched April sleep on the couch and, as they ate dinner, her world shimmered and shook, and a tiny fissure, a patch of black, opened up. This thing she had done had made a hole in the universe. She looked around the room: her dad's ear was gone and where April should be lying on the couch was darkness. The blankets gathered and wrinkled like there was no body there. Nothing.

Nic ate her dinner slowly, wary of this world plunged half into dark. She moved food around the plate. She blinked, rubbed her eyes. She looked over at April again, at the place where April should be, and it was like she'd never been there. Nic pressed her hands into her thighs beneath the table at the thought.

'She's just sleeping,' aunt Grace said and reached over and rubbed Nic's back a little. 'She'll be fine.'

Nic blinked, let herself be gently nudged back into the room and the world resolved after a time but the feeling remained. The adults talked and didn't try to draw her in. She noticed the green of the peas, the smell of the butter from the mash, and the blood leaking from the small piece of steak she'd been given. She moved things around a bit more with her arms and her head grew so heavy.

She must have fallen asleep right there at the table. Her dad lifted her and carried her up the stairs. Put her to sleep in Grace's bed. Her body was heavy and everything was dark and thick. And then April was in bed beside her; he'd carried her up too and he laid her on her back so her wound wouldn't touch the pillow or have any pressure on it. She was returned. Nic reached out and took her sister's hand and held it all night.

'I love you,' April said in the morning. 'Even though you

tried to kill me.'

Nic squeezed her hand. 'Why didn't you duck?'

CHAPTER 4

In the long Scottish summer half-light, Star was crying. She'd been crying non-stop since they put her out of their bed and into her own bed. Her crying rattled the small cradle she was in and little reverberations hit Nic and Charlie in bed. They felt like tremors. Nic gave in and brought her daughter back into bed and tried to quiet her, then tried to get her to feed, but she was agitated and right crabbit. Nic's breasts were full and sore and a hot ridge marked the right one: a blockage, pre-mastitis, and she took a finger and tried to work it through. Her teeth ached with the sharp soreness of it, up around her jaw. She shivered and Star seemed to take that on board, turned her head away with a force that surprised Nic. Beside her Charlie gave her space. She'd bitten his head off at some point for annoying her while feeding and now kept a distance she regretted creating.

After another time, minutes, an hour, who could tell— the screaming bent time and space—Charlie got out of bed and took the baby from her. He walked a small path along the side of the bed. Star began a new pattern. She screamed until she choked, then gulped and gasped and fell into a worrying silence before embarking once again on her disquieting round: the distinct shapes of degrees of infant crisis all severe-to-gale-force and tonight. If Nic were to rate it, she'd say violent storm force eleven.

Finn showed up at his parents' bedroom door. He watched his dad and the baby with his hands over his ears.

'I know, Fisher, I know.' Charlie put his finger to his lips.

They'd not been sure the bed was a good idea because it gave Finn so much freedom to roam and soon he'd be able to work the child's gate at the top of the stairs and they'd need to be vigilant.

'Let's let your mother sleep.'

But Nic lifted the covers slightly and Finn leaned in, she snuggled him, kissed his cheek, pushed his dark curls back from his face.

Charlie, still holding their daughter, guided their son back to bed. Finn climbed in and smoothed the covers along his legs and over his body and lay down. A thing he did. But he was a messy sleeper and he'd be tussled and in a sheet-fankle within minutes of sleep taking him. He wasn't ready for that yet and sat back up. He looked to his dad who held his daughter close, thinking his heart beat might soothe her, but Star was still not calm. His son's look said, *Do something, please.*

Charlie lay Star down on the bed, opened the thin cotton

blanket she was wrapped in and began to swaddle her. Finn watched, reaching out his hand to touch his sister. 'It's okay, Star, it'll be okay.' He patted her arm. 'Shhh. You'll feel better if you sleep.'

From the mouth of babes; all the things they told him.

Charlie pulled the blanket snug. Tuck. Snug. Tuck. Snug tuck. He whispered to her, a few Gaelic words, a few Scots ones too, which wrapped around her. Finn said sweet beautiful things to his sister too. Nothing. Just words. Joyful words.

'Samhradh,' said Charlie.

'Summer,' Finn said, translating.

'Sun Broch,' Charlie said, his mother's words in his mouth.

'Ray of sun,' his son translated, temporarily taking his hand from beneath the covers to flit his fingers through the air, angling down to touch the blanket around his sister.

'Star,' said Charlie.

'Star.'

And Charlie held up the blanket and Finn re-tucked in. A thankful snuggle in, eyelids heavier.

'Cake.'

'Fairy.'

'Chocolate.'

'Buttons,' said Nic so they could hear. She should've been

sleeping, but she was listening.

'Chocolate Buttons!' shouted Finn.

'Enough,' Charlie said. 'Sleeping.'

His cheeky boy added, 'zzzzzzzzzzs' and then 'story.'

When Nic and Charlie's daughter was born, in the late spring, a few months ago, Nic's family chuckled when they heard that name.

'A Star is born!'

Nic and Charlie would hear that a lot but it didn't dissuade them from her name, Star. On the birth certificate her name was Chrissie Avens-Skirving but Nic wasn't ready to share that information yet—not to her parents or her sister or her brother or the nurses whose laughing eyes said more than enough. The tame, conformist capitulation written on the form would be between her and Charlie and the registrar. Out here in the real world, let people think what they will.

'What's her middle name, Burst?' Grace asked, getting in on the hilarity, standing beside Nic who was propped up in the hospital bed with her daughter small and emergent in her arms.

'Ship Enterprise, actually,' Nic answered as she lifted her daughter up. Grace kissed Star and made baby noises. She bent her arms and with the infant within them she brought her close to her body. Small fast breaths together. She touched her nose: 'Aren't you a cutie?' She bestowed the gentlest of kisses upon her forehead and because he was antsy and desperate to hold his granddaughter, Grace passed Star to Sonny.

Nic's dad scooped her up and cooed, 'My little starship, my little starship.' Kissed her. Grinned. Kissed her again.

A few months later, Star was still a tiny one-arm deal and Charlie held her in his left arm and leant over his son, smoothing the covers, even after Finn had done it himself. A muscle memory. Nic said her dad still slept like that. Sheet, blanket, thin duvet, all neat and tucked around him. Unlike Finn, he'd be in exactly the same place when he woke. Nic said she didn't know how he did it. The snoring alone should cause ripples and fractures.

Charlie started the story as he always did, *'Out at the furthest jut of rocks on a long beach that stretches out into a wide burst of water to the west, just after a late spring sun was setting even further out, beyond where the eye can know what it is, even though we know it's the sun, we're flying through space and turning and the sun is hot explosive at its centre and yet when it reaches us it's warm. Tonight as this boy looks out over the water, light shimmers in the sky green and pink and looks like the sparkly toy they ask him to hand to his younger sister to distract her when they're in the middle of doing*

*a task like chopping wood or kneading bread or talking to uncle Ben
on the phone that means they can't see to her right away, and she loves
those colours and the way they move.*

*His dad had taught him to wish upon falling stars and to
breathe in the Northern Lights. Above them the sky is alive and his
mum laughs as she opens her arms, his dad too, and they laugh and
turn and when they need air they breathe in and the boy can see their
breath enter their bodies as light. They shimmer. The boy breathes in
too and although he can't see his belly and lungs light up, he knows
they have. The small family stays there all night, leaning back on
their rucksacks and covering themselves with spare jumpers, ignoring
bedtime and needing a roof overhead because the lights are rare and
you make time for rare things. And in the morning he walks home,
holding his mother's hand on one side, his father's hand on the other,
and each time they lift him clear of small obstacles, a rock or a big
clump of heather, he feels the lights in their grip. And can see them
all a-light each time they smile, each time they look at him and say,*
Please, Finn, please go to sleep. Please eat your peas. Please give
your sister a kiss and tell her you love her.'

Finn dropped off in no time. Charlie didn't know how much he
heard. He simply wanted to be settled by someone who loved

him. Star remained restless in Charlie's arms and he walked with her tentatively, getting used to this new child. He walked barefoot out of Finn's bedroom, and a few times along the short corridor that ran between each room. And then light steps down the stairs. He did a circuit and then another in the kitchen and living room and finally slid his feet into wellies with a small squelch for they were last worn in last night's deluge. He went outside. The air held traces of the thick fog that bound them earlier but even now the deep blue sky was infused with a faint midsummer light. Charlie could see where he walked, and this croft of theirs still looked to him like untamed land, despite all their efforts.

'It will be a home for all of us,' he said to Star. She was asleep now, and it wouldn't matter that he'd used the future tense instead of pretending it was true already. He walked around the edges of their land, near enough its boundaries; their ten acres, no, it was Nic's ten acres, although she'd long since stopped bringing that truth to his or anyone else's attention. Heading for the water, or close enough, Star slept deeply and wouldn't wake again and so he was walking only for himself.

His new daughter. This, his life.

As he opened the door to the house, a pale daylight grew outside. Just inside, he pressed the toes of one foot against the heel of the other and prised the first wellie off. It clumped to the floor.

Then the other, with a bare foot this time. Clump. He walked quietly up the stairs and into the bedroom, imagining Nic and him unencumbered.

Into the cot Star went for a second time. A risk, sure, but he did it anyway. Nic was asleep, but lightly, and made room. He stripped down, his trousers and shirt making a loose pile on the floor. His cool cheek against her hot one. She had stripped down too, mid-night, because they'd not changed over to the summer duvet. She was always so hot to the touch and they joked about it—how she felt the cold, got cold, and yet was so hot beside him. The pregnancies had transformed her body. She'd shirked off the curves between the pregnancies and he didn't miss them, didn't not miss them. It was amazing how one body could produce another, that a body could be that generous, change its shape that much. She settled her new body along the lines of his own, which was also thickening, strengthening. They shifted and settled. She didn't move her hands down. She wasn't quite ready for that.

April and Col had not come up for air and this breathlessness was new to them both. April had an old scar on her forehead; Col had scars with equally interesting stories. And somehow, in the way they touched, in the tenderness, intensity, and care, they didn't need to speak about their histories, the choices they'd made and, each minute, enacted.

The cake rose and cooled and the frosting was thick and sweet and buttery, and Grace devoured it with homemade mint ice-cream and was three dream worlds away by now. Here she was undertaking a long walk on Skye, out to the Maidens on a hot summer's day with a belly full of ache. In her dream her stepmother Suzie was dead and her gorgeous Max too, a death that ended her five-year closeted affair with the singer. Her grief was bold and the world heaved and tilted and spun. She moved with a leaden slowness. The strength of it all threatened her ability to walk and navigate and so she slowed down. Eventually, when she needed it, a white-tailed eagle skimmed the cliff edge and circled above, lingering as if only for her. Half a mile further along, a juvenile golden eagle flew alongside the cliffs with strong white patches visible beneath each wing, and then it flew alongside her for a little while. *Thank you*, she said. *Thank you both.*

On her way back her sister appeared on a clump of heather, standing with her hands on her hips, chin jutted forward. 'Aye, get over it,' she said. 'Move on. That's life.' Her difficult, estranged sister, Viv. What right did she have?

'Fuck you,' Grace said.

Viv laughed and made a rude gesture. 'You stay away from my kids!' but didn't come any closer. That was fresh, Viv saying that, when she'd not been there for them and her kids felt her absence every day and hung onto fury and indifference and hope about their mother, Grace knew, despite what they might say. At least two of them wanted their mother to come back so she'd be accountable for all the crap she'd left them with. They didn't know Viv like she did and she'd never own up to any of it. Personally, Grace thought that a true, reliable absence might be better than the complicated presence her sister was sure to bring. Grace walked by her sister, making a rude gesture of her own, and out of the corner of her eye she saw Viv turn into a stunning display of yellow-orange gorse. Grace's anger flared and then settled the further she walked on, and at the end of the walk she didn't know what to feel—grief, joy or a fiery hot resentful anger.

Sonny got up and made himself a cup of tea and grabbed two chocolate biscuits. He knew he shouldn't; all the books on insomnia recommended against it, but he did it anyway. He sat in the dark and looked out as day and night skirted each other like timid partners on a dance floor. It was hard to tell which was advancing and which was giving way.

His hands ached from the past weeks of work and he thought of how he liked to fix things that were broken. When he was with an engine or a machine, he was with it, and looked no further. He knew he should plan more, but never could. It was a problem, had always been a problem. He had got Viv pregnant. Took the first job that came his way despite the bellyache he had about it. His speciality changed from the workings of machines to the mechanics of weapons, and the strain of it produced an ulcer and high blood pressure.

Sonny had continued to work for violent men and take his family to dangerous places, and he knew what they'd seen when he couldn't shield them because he'd seen it too. Everyday things in all sorts of countries. The poverty was standard and difficult and something they had a taste of themselves as a family, but it was the threat of violence in almost all cities on almost all streets that each move spotlighted. Boys with guns; men, who were just big boys, with guns. Women and girls three steps behind or not seen at all. This was in the east, west, north and south; in less developed countries and those that think they're leaders in all things. In the midst of it, he simply tried to survive. You could take on the worst of a thing, be cowed or twisted by something that felt too big to impact or change. Viv tried to effect change but her efforts were a handful of sand thrown into a lake, not even causing a ripple. Her attempts in each community they moved to were both terrifying and incredible. Sexy. Even now he longed for Viv. He drank tea and tried to remember the women he'd dated since and confused names and faces and details. Tiredness approached and he noted it.

Puffing up one of the pillows he had on the couch, which had come with the house and smelled faintly of sweat, he knew if he walked even the short way to bed the urge to sleep would abandon him. He slid down and bent his knees so he fit on the couch and soon he was dreaming of the gears of the first car he ever fixed, when he was fourteen, with his dad giving helpful pointers but never intervening. His dad in this familiar dream was only a voice and indeed this was the only way Sonny ever remembered him. His mum walking back towards their house, emerging from the path that led up from the firth. She had on a loose skirt which flapped in the wind, with their chocolate Labrador beside her, off the lead despite the nesting birds.

With a turn of the key, the engine caught and it was a glorious sound. His dad whooped. Sonny climbed behind the wheel, his mother got in beside him and his dad and the dog in the back. They drove through the quick Highland roads, this country his parents had each chosen, and over the radio 'Wild Mountain Thyme' came on and they belted it out. Sonny tried to stop the dream here but it played on. The car expanded like a lung taking in oxygen and the rest of his family appeared. First Viv, then Grace, and then each of his children too—Ben, April and Nic all laughing out to him, to his parents and to the world. As their speed increased, the car transformed rapidly from one thing to another into distorted versions of: all the pokey unsatisfying places he'd ever lived with his family, of this weapon or this machine he'd built or fixed. The car turned into an open hand that slowly curled in its fingers, threatening his family held in the palm and all of them shouting, *Dad! Sonny! Stop this. Make it stop.* And then people he loved vanished: first his dad, then his mum, then Grace and Viv, and he looked back, the world fluttering and shiny like it was viewed through a prism, and one by one his children left him too.

When the car was empty, Sonny's eyes opened and from his horizontal position he saw mid-summer slowly bringing colour to the sky and trees, which emerged rose-red in the building light. He lay for the next few hours, memories spooling and looping, heart racing and aching, watching as the longest day of the year came into its own.

Ben had an ice pack on his cheek and a bust lip. His knuckle was raw and sweet with contact.

CHAPTER 5

Summers at Grace's cottage were the idyll in the midst of an unpredictable, errant, hard-working life that took them all around the world, not in a glamorous fashion, but in a Sonny-will-fixit-cut-rate sort of way, and here's your crappy one-bedroom apartment for your family of five. He exposed his family to such risk and it was the pressures of his job, the moral hinterland he chose to live and work in, that made the summers at Grace's—with the cacophony of the place, the very green of the woods, the light, life and appeal of routine—so important.

When the kids were young, Grace entertained them. She took Ben swimming in the loch and conjured boundless energy to play with the girls when they were toddlers; letting the girls come into her bedroom and jump up and down on her bed so Sonny and Viv could get some sleep.

During the summer Ben was hardly ever in the house, and when he was he'd be dripping onto Grace's floor, her laying towels out for him to wrap himself in, wiping up the footprints, but he didn't notice them or the water that clung to him and would plop down on the couch, divesting himself of the loch he'd carried into her house. The words out of her mouth: a brief moment of aunting or mothering and of pleasure as well as annoyance.

One summer, on a scorcher of a day—sunny and hot and unbearable in the small house and the claustrophobic woods—Sonny and Ben tugged on their T-shirts to get air between their sweat-sticky shirts and their slick chests—their faces red, the air still and the midges gathering, noting easy, juicy prey. Ben started to make a move towards the door and the water beyond that. He was already in his swimming trunks. As an eleven-year-old boy, he more or less lived in them on the outside chance there'd be the possibility of going for a swim.

'Can I join you?' Sonny asked. It was strange to ask his son for permission but it felt right; Sonny was definitely asking to tag along. Ben nodded and went outside, waited for Sonny to change. Sonny expected them to head for Belter's Loch but Ben turned them west and north, leading the way along a narrow path through the woods towards the dunes and to a deep long sea loch.

'Do you come here on your own?'

Ben hesitated, nodded.

'How far do you swim?'

He pointed far out. 'Until I get tired.'

'What about the return trip?'

'I like the challenge.'

Sonny pushed down the urge to nag him. 'That what you want to do today?'

'Yeah. We'll swim until you get tired.'

'And you'll just hang back, take it easy on me.'

'Old man,' he laughed out of nowhere, 'you'll not outswim me.'

There was a slight in that comment, that Sonny wasn't up to the task of beating his son in a simple swim, and it was a dare he accepted. Sonny didn't take it easy or pretend to go slower and his lungs grew sharp with a need for oxygen and his legs burned with the effort and, although Ben was looking a bit tired, he had another distance in him before he would have stopped. The suddenness of an osprey fishing just ahead of them stopped them both. The bird emerged from the water, a fish catapulting its body back and forth in a futile attempt to escape, the bird shaking water from its wings as it gained altitude. They slid onto their backs, floated and watched the sky. There was no easy exchange but only shared space. His son, reserved even then, was overly sensitive. Eventually, Ben spiralled in the water onto his front, started kicking and headed back to shore.

Out on the water each day that week, they would swim, float, swim. It was a mercurial sea loch, but in a country of few lightning storms, they were never put off their swim by the weather.

Ben and Sonny continued to swim in silence; his son's lips often prickled into a grimace that reminded him of his wife. There were already lines emerging around his eyes that didn't settle and a skinniness was creeping in—a sign that he often forgot to eat. He grew skinny when he was fifteen, tried to slit his wrists and Nic, who was only eleven, had covered for him. Even Sonny knew. How could he not know?

'He was trying to fix his bed, so it didn't creak so much when he pulled it out. And a sharp spring caught his wrist.' Nic put a hand on Sonny's shoulder as he looked at Ben's injury.

Sonny looked at the wound, the straight line of it, along the artery. Thankfully not quite deep enough, not quite long enough. Plus, when had Ben tried to fix anything around the house, ever?

'That'll teach you to help out around here,' Sonny said, trying to catch his son's eyes. His daughter squeezed his shoulder.

Ben nodded, 'Lesson learned.' But his eyes were on Nic, all on Nic. As Sonny turned to get more bandages, a butterfly or two, he knew Ben had mouthed to Nic, *Thank you, Thank you.*

When Ben was nineteen, he was tanned, and a stalky, spindly sort of strong. He'd already started college and dropped out, as each of Sonny's kids would do, and had been labouring on farms throughout Europe in exchange for room and board.

While the physical nature of these jobs seemed to suit him, like swimming did, his jaw was held too tightly and he looked scrawny. That's what indecisiveness did to a young man. His son needed to stop fannying about, worrying about things he couldn't change.

Out on the water, as a light drizzle fell, they were a young man and a middle-aged man floating on their backs for a while, looking at the blue sky expanding that would soon chase away the rain. A rest before heading back.

Sonny felt that inaction was the worst thing of all. Do something. It had to be better than letting life do what it would with you. That would never end well.

'I'm thinking, Ben, that you should think about your next steps. Have you thought about joining the military? Or doing something you can be respected for?' He had tried to leave it open, so Ben could say what he wanted to say, do what he'd like. But Sonny knew as soon as the words were out of his mouth that his tone was all wrong. He heard it, how the implication of his question was closed. He heard the unreasonableness of asking a nineteen-year-old who clearly didn't know his own mind about the colour of his swimming trunks much less a direction in life. His was a statement of his disappointment in his son. Sonny was disappointed and couldn't deny it and couldn't correct his tone. Ben was so capable and he wasn't moving forward. Look at those shoulders, the speed of him and the strength: he could be something.

'A job like you had?'

'I didn't say that.'

Ben shook his head, turned towards his dad and treaded water. 'Once I figured out what you did, I was scared for you. I had a right to be scared for you and for us. And yet you took us all with you. To all those places.'

They shared experiences of witnessing poverty, and violence, but that's the world and it's better his kids knew it. 'It was fine. I took care of myself and of you. I wanted to keep the family together.'

'Look how well that worked. You've got yourself a nice, stable nuclear family.' Sarcasm wasn't gracious and he'd raised Ben better than that, but his son continued. 'And now you want me to do what?'

'Something. Anything. Seriously, Ben, you're fighting me on this?'

His arrogance infuriated Sonny and he'd headed for shore in a huff, which was a mistake, as his stronger, angrier son overtook him swiftly and smoothly. Ben held nothing back and was out of the water and striding along the path before Sonny was even halfway to shore.

That night Ben laughed with his sisters as normal and left in the morning, as he'd been planning to do. Sonny felt that fracture alongside the thinner camaraderie with Grace and his family retreated from him as if he were an ogre.

Ben disappeared for a few years and returned as a trained engineer working on the rigs, and although the travel increased, so did his wages. Sonny was glad. He'd have more structure, support, rules. It'd be good for him. But then Sonny watched. Ben put weight back on, but it was a shining sort of bulk and nothing about him looked happier. After that, on the occasions they managed a few days at Grace's, Ben was back at the smaller, freshwater Belter Loch for short swims alone. Sonny couldn't be sure it was intentional but his son was never in the room alone with him, never in a place where he might say, *Son, are you happy? What can I do to help?*

CHAPTER 6

Sixty flights. Who could have predicted that? Ben's last journey in a dodgy metal bird. He was done. Finally finished with it all and he was lucky not to have the police waiting in a car at the docks. Jock, the rig foreman, had been really clear about this.

'Get some help,' he'd whispered. 'I have a brother like you and he's six years into a twenty-year sentence.'

Ben had clenched and unclenched his fists by his side as this huge man leaned in and did him a favour, however patronising his manner. Only Ben's deep respect for Jock had stopped him exercising his fists again. The knuckles of both hands were already roughed-up with the thumping he'd just given.

Despite a hint of generosity, Jock had been clear in his decisions and swift. At midnight Ben had punched Andy and hadn't stopped when asked politely and still hadn't stopped when two guys were holding his arms, thereby forcing him to use his feet and yet, even with a swollen lip and an eye turning raised and bruised, after all that Andy had still chosen to be an arsehole with a big mouth.

'He's a fucking good-for-nothing,' he'd shouted and spat,

looking towards Grant who was gaunt and using the railing to hold himself up. 'They're all covering for him,' he said. And then, pointing then at Ben, 'This darkie is the worst.'

Maybe it was this last bit that saved Ben: Andy was a nasty racist piece of work as well as being the type who treated you like shite, didn't show up for his shift, or did a shoddy job, but then tried to put it on you, or make you feel bad for him by saying he has a heart condition or was pre-diabetic whereas really he rushed and was not very good at his job. He was a braggart and a bully. Many of the guys had wanted to let rip at Andy themselves. Ben was well-liked on the rig because he'd look out for you, he was diligent and never made excuses.

'Ben's lucky that Andy isn't on the flight with him or on his way to the hospital,' Jock said loudly, so all the guys heard him, as he ushered Ben onto the deck and into the waiting helicopter. His hand was solid, like a brother's, on Ben's back. 'Good luck,' he said and they shook hands before Ben sat on board with the other broken, unsalvageable parts.

Three in the morning and Grant, who had been puking up for over a week and been too weak to get out of his bunk, was buckled in next to Ben with a bucket gripped in both hands on his lap. Grant was really sick in a way he'd known about for months, in a way that he'd not told the bosses, in a way never confirmed by the doctors, but he knew it. All the guys knew it and had been trying to cover for him, because they knew he needed this job. The two had been close friends for years. Grant had a wife he was crazy about, four kids, a sick dad, a strung-out sister who had three kids and an out-of-work alcoholic husband, and no one had any hidden resources. The whole family was tapped out, used up, and now Grant was jobless. That's what the fight had been about. Andy had been going to rat Grant out to the bosses as a lazy so-and-so. Ben threatened him, ever so briefly with words and then lightning-quick with his fists. Since Ben had two warnings already, that was him off the rigs, out of a job, and, finally, on his last flight over the water. He put a hand on Grant's shoulder, who winced, his whole body in constant pain, and it was clear that he'd be dead in a few days or weeks or months because he'd worked far past the point he could be helped. Grant had thrown everything into life and was going to lose it. Ben's position was less honourable. Ben had simply failed as everyone had expected him to and now he was in this helicopter with the garbage and his near-dead friend and there was nothing out of place in the whole world.

A sweet sharp tightening pinched in his chest. There. There it was again. Still. That sharp grip. What he deserved. What he brought on himself. The familiar exhilaration surged as a gust of wind blasted them and pushed the helicopter to the side which then it righted itself. It wasn't the flying he hated but something else the flying roused in him. How the risk of life was made obvious each minute in this piece of tin. The catch was fast and sudden, and then his breath was freed, his chest recovered and he moved on. Grant looked at him, noticing, maybe.

Each moment of each flight brought a surge of adrenalin that tricked him with its bright, false charge, but the racing was really a churning—thick and murky—and each experience of it took days from his life. He brought his hand to his chest: open into the air, closed in the tap. Understanding this, almost as soon as he started the job, he'd marked each flight in each rattling machine. He more or less carved the first days taken by hand into his arm, always when on shore leave, in his damp little flat, sitting on his own, crap movie on the telly, beer open. Intentional lines of punctures, a black-brown ink pushed down as far as he could get it, just darker than his skin up the inside of his arm, first covering the old scar and then moving up towards his elbow. When Sonia moved in, he'd do it in a corner of the dockside pub when they first landed, while the guys watched, egging him on.

'Deeper, Ben.'

'Don't you go hitting a vein. Who'll they'll get to replace you?'

He looked up, still eyes, serious. 'Dozens of guys could take my place.'

The other punters, all replaceable too, nodded and drank their beer. Truth.

When they landed, Ben helped Grant onto the tarmac. He'd expected an ambulance to be waiting, but only a small Ford Escort was parked there, with Molly sitting behind the wheel. She emerged—pregnant, Ben noticed, baby number five—and rushed to take Grant's other arm. Together they got him into the passenger seat. Ben mumbled apologies to Molly and to Grant.

'I tried,' Ben said, his eyes down, body defeated.

'There's nothing for it, mate,' Grant said.

Molly failed to hold back tears but was silent, simply letting them fall, as she moved with an efficient practicality familiar to Ben from the days he'd spent with the family. It wasn't clear whether Ben's actions had protected Grant, given him more time with his family, or hastened his departure.

'If there's anything I can do…' said Ben.

Molly nodded, once, still looking at her husband. Ben couldn't read her face or his and with both doors closed he just made out her saying, *We're all so glad you're coming home.*

Here he was again, choosing what he didn't want to do. He didn't want to be on the rigs and so he'd manufactured a sufficient departure. Just like he hadn't wanted to go to university and sit behind a desk in a city so he hadn't bothered to get the grades he needed. And he certainly hadn't wanted to carry a gun, or use one, or help anyone else carry a gun, and so he avoided anything with a military edge. When he was eighteen he had been toying with the idea until one drunken night at Grace's, April and Nic had helped him see that it was a stupid idea, using those exact words. 'Just don't. You know it, I know it, the walls know it.'

'I know it too,' shouted Grace from the stairs outside where she sat with her whisky, cigarette and girlfriend of the moment.

Behind his sisters' statements were the clear memories of things they'd witnessed and how they knew their dad had colluded in order to survive. He'd done the things his employers asked him to do, and in the process he took his family to all the nooks and crannies the world had forgotten about, except those who saw the opportunity to plunder all resources, be they natural or human, and his kids had witnessed simple acts of indignity against the poor and women and children and those who were a different religion or faith or race. Ben thought that brutal acts against women seemed to be something that was simply allowed no matter where they went. He thought it but didn't know how to change it; but he thought he knew how to not contribute to it. This had been part of the reason not to go into the air force or the navy or the army. Enough of a reason.

He thought he'd been choosing wisely, but avoiding one wrong decision doesn't mean the next one will be right and it wasn't long before Ben was out on the rigs doing nothing in the world that was much use but, he thought, wouldn't do much harm. But eventually he realised his job was the backbone of the petrochemical military industrial complex. He was part of the problem, just as his dad was part of the problem. Actions. Collusion. And now he here he was, jobless, purposeless and he wasn't sure what he could do to keep people safe—his own people, other people, anyone, himself.

Sally was smoking in front of the shop. He'd texted her and she was waiting, even at this hour. She reached out and touched his cheek, beside the cuts and the bruises. Raised an eyebrow, let her hand fall to his shoulder where she rested it, slowly moving it onto his back to guide him inside. She gave him two more inked marks—one vertical, one diagonal. He was an inmate marking days. She tapped the inside of his elbow.

'That's me, finished,' he said.

'Me too.'

'No, I mean, I got the boot today. I won't be back.'

She smiled, maybe thinking of the extra sleep she'd get, maybe thinking he should have done it months or years ago. 'Right then. It's been what it's been, Ben.'

'Yes.'

With a bandage on his wrist, a butterfly plaster holding his eye together, and a duffle bag slung across his back, he headed for the bus station and with every step the world lost structure. The fabric of himself unraveled and started to re-assemble. He was six foot four with dark hair and skin, which he got from both sides. His mother had an engineering student grandfather she mentioned only once, who was from Ghana. He couldn't stand the cold damp Scottish weather and left behind a pretty girlfriend and colicky baby.

Too early to text Nic. But he'd call her later. Maybe Finn would be there and he'd give a wee shout and dance in the background. *Ben Ben Ben Butt 'n' Ben*. Maybe after a couple of days at Grace's with the whole family, Nic and Charlie would invite him up to their house, give him the foldout bed in the living room, and let him rest and mend and make his way forward.

Sleep had taken the rest of Ben's family. Through open windows the mid-summer long-dawn chorus continued and the faintest lights flickered at the edges of what could be known.

CHAPTER 7

Ruined

The summer April was seventeen—when they'd all come to Grace's for their annual family holiday, after a night sneaking out and drinking in the pub, when her sister and brother had left at a reasonable hour and April insisted on staying until last orders, and then going out dancing for a bit, insisting that no one would notice that her tent was empty—April brought a boy back with her to the woods. Not to Grace's cottage exactly, but nearby. She directed him to park his car on the road and she extended the hand that had been on his thigh during the drive and led him through the night woods up towards the dilapidated stone buildings that sat just under the brow of the hill.

On their short journey through the trees she discovered that it's not only girls who can be afraid in the woods in the dark. Although this boy didn't stay anything, his hand in hers grew sweaty and shook with faint tremors. With him in this state she wasn't sure they'd make it to the top and so halfway up she stopped and let him come in close. Her hands on him; his hands on her. She leaned back against a tree, and he pressed her further against it. She pushed back and their kissing became a tussle of sorts, unfurled and re-bounded with more need and he sort of tackled her then, to bring her down to the ground. A friendly, playful tackle, but a display of force and direction. She let him have it. But took it back by taking off her trousers, and his too, and wrestling again for the upper hand. If there was any doubt in him it vanished then, and they became a mess of limbs amidst the leaves and fallen cones and pine needles.

Some people liked the chase, mind games, toys. She'd heard all sorts at school. April learned here, with this boy, that she liked to fuck in the woods. She liked the equal footing it gave her. It may not have been so equal in just any woods, but here in her woods—these trees, these places she believed she knew at any time of day and night here in the summer—this was easy and she had no fear. They both came to, standing under their own steam, and found and then adjusted their clothes. They did make it to the top of the hill with April leading the way, scaring a deer away from the ruins. Doubt shone out of his eyes and it seemed as if he looked around for any sharp objects she might have hidden, any signs that she might be mad or dangerous. Only witches screw you like that.

They drank a bottle of beer each, from the stash she and

Nic had kept hidden in the half-collapsed fireplace of the ruin every year since they were fourteen (and from which Ben often stole and never replaced). The boy stood where the front archway had been and had one foot outside the threshold as he raced through his drink.

'You want a lift back?' he asked, almost like a gentleman might.

'No, I'll walk from here.'

'Oh, okay. I'll just make my own way back to the car then,' he said, 'it's not far.'

A statement but also a question.

'No, not far,' April assured him but didn't guide or follow. She heard the snapping of branches and the brush of bracken as he didn't so much walk as half-run down the hill. He should take a wee bit more care, she was thinking, and then she heard it, the trip and the halt. But he wasn't timid, not really, just on unfamiliar territory and he got up quickly and continued on. Not in the right direction, April noted, but he didn't stop moving.

April stepped over the crumbled wall and into a small clearing, dropped her jeans and peed, then righted herself and drank another beer sitting on the ruin. It wasn't long before he came back, disorientated and unsure. She had a head torch stuffed into her coat pocket, although she rarely used it and certainly not on a clear night like tonight. She led him down a faint and broken path to his car. She didn't know if he looked up the hill to see if he could figure out the path, or if he noticed the slight break in the trees that held an abandoned cottage, visible from the road if you knew where to look. If you weren't impulsive and perhaps a bit fearful, not paying attention, you might never realise you could see the path from the road when the light hit it right.

She'd already started towards Grace's when she heard the turn of the engine call out into the night, around a corner or behind a tree beyond what she could see. She heard, too, her brother and sister laughing over in the loch, the water-babies, the best friends. She didn't hear Grace who had been known to join them for the swims; hell, she's the one who showed them the magnificence of it. But it was only Nic and Ben swimming far out in the water, laughing, telling stories and floating on their backs, looking up at the sky, a bluish white from the full moon, and just now, by seconds and degrees, expanding into the tempered light of morning.

CHAPTER 8

A slim five hours after their dance, rain chucked it down in a burst of cold, and April and Col shared a quick coffee, legs entwined, out on her front steps, glad of the faint breeze that kept the midges at bay. Col had a meeting up near Ullapool, had to get going and wouldn't take the jacket April offered.

'I'm alright,' Col said and sprinted down the hill, making a new path that was slightly more direct and rocky. Col was surefooted and quickly disappeared into the trees.

She stood on the path outside her house and listened to the early morning. This place was often loud. Burgeoning and peopled, for she had other neighbours to both sides, within partial line of sight. She liked being a part of a small community. Today was relatively still and she heard the crack of twigs and heather beneath Col's feet and then, only when that grew quiet and disappeared, did other movements rise to the surface. The sheep moving down from the hill, an inexorable approach of white dots. The cuckoo, the precious cuckoo, calling from the tree near the burn. The sound of a car on the road.

Her first morning in this house had been the first day

of a thaw, in the first week of April, and she'd stood in the sun and listened to the litany of noises: birdsong, a neighbour's outrageously barking dogs, a sheep's baa'ing, and the punctuation of the woodpecker's thrum. She almost sat and lit up a cigarette as a way to enjoy the moment, but thought *this is the new me*, and resisted even though she knew she was the same as before and brought all her disasters with her: a mistaken hook up; the times her mouth got her into trouble; the time she was fired from a job she hated and wasn't suited for; the time she'd fallen on her arse.

She thought of herself as a good girl in bad girl's jeans. Mostly she was invisible, until the overwhelming need to provoke overtook her. The need to take up space. To not be sorry. The world wanted her to be sorry. Wanted all girls everywhere to be sorry. All the women in the world. Well, she said no to that. Her mum had taught her that too with the way she'd fought against their dad, fighting for them, but he couldn't see it, and, despite her wilful absence from their lives, April knew she owed her mum a lot. There's learning to be had in watching a disaster play out before your eyes. Nic and Ben didn't agree, and vilified Viv. Nic because she'd abandoned them all and had stayed so completely and arrogantly out of contact; Ben because he despised her behaviour—even the anxiety and rage he had too—turning what Viv had done over and over in his head, and it never lost any of its heat.

When April had showed up in the Strath at her Aunt Grace's door, twenty years old, with a temporary black eye and a more persistent depression, Grace shook her head. 'That Viv, that Viv.' As if her mother was to blame for the world's problems.

'Don't,' April said. 'A racist drunk at the bar gave me the shiner and, for the rest of it, I'm too old to lay this at Mum's feet.' She paused, shrugging. 'Even if any of us knew where those feet were.'

A pause and they both laughed. 'If you can crack that joke then you can help me with this fence.' It was a blunt, obvious attempt to get April outdoors and out of her funk. 'Best to learn ways to navigate times like these when you're young,' Grace said, 'or they'll have you in their grip forever. They might do anyway but, you never know, it's worth a shot.'

It worked well enough for April, and after the fence it was the garden, and then her neighbour Siobhan's decking, then helping to fill the potholes in the 1/2-mile-long drive of another neighbour, and that's how April shifted her dog days enough to stay out of bed for a few hours at a time, and make herself useful, and this is how she made a living the first year here, and for many years after.

April had never run before she came to this place and even now most times she'd head out saying to herself it'd be a walk; she'd simply let herself shift her stride if the urge appeared. She only ever wanted to run here in the woods and never in the city or on the coast. These forest paths posed a challenge, and one she liked.

She'd expected to be asleep this morning at this time but she was up, full-body awake, and so she put on her running gear and headed out. Her house key went in the tiny zipped pocket and she carried nothing else.

The forest was really many different parcels of land—woods, high moorland, bogs—all connected by paths—human, deer and vehicular—and sectioned off by fences, some of them easier to cross than others, April had come to find.

You could get lost in these woods, and she had, although it was more a feeling of disorientation, really, because there were many hills and curves and the perspective could change so quickly that something familiar looked foreign.

She walked through the open patch of ground she and her neighbours' shared, a diffuse early light showing the grass green and tufted. As soon as she hit the path at the edge of the woods, she picked up her pace. Weaving a way uphill, April stepped over fallen branches, the heather and blaeberries and bracken brushing her legs as she ducked beneath low-hanging branches, now heavy with leaves, flowers and berries. She'd cleared this narrow track over the last few months and her movements kept some of the summer growth at bay. Her breath was loud in her ears in a still and quiet world, and the trees were whispering sentinels, hardly roused in an occasional, barely there breeze.

She ran above and past her Aunt Grace's house, which was dark and full of sleep. Smart woman. April would see her later as she'd had promised to help paint her fence. It'd become a yearly ritual and April knew Grace's cottage and its boundaries well, as it'd been a waystation of sorts before April found her feet again. Even as the cottage was dark, she wondered if Grace looked out into the world and watched her niece pass.

A bit further on April could see the bungalow her dad started to rent a few months ago. The house was an ugly thing, built in the '70s, but functional and affordable and surprisingly close to April and Grace. Almost as if each of them were coming to consider it home.

She'd text her dad in an hour or two to see if he could drive her to where her car sat in the community hall's car park. Hopefully he'd not ask any questions, but she was sure he would serious-joke that he might have to charge her for the diesel he used. He kept a small, neat notebook in the glove compartment and marked down his mileage, how much fuel he put in the tank, and worked out not only his mileage, manually, but split his usage into personal, favours, and business trips. April took it as a point of pride that she did not have her own column in his notebook, yet. It proved she was an adult. Adulting.

Although there were no lights on, he would already be up. It was the military man in him. The hard worker. Him with his shoulders squared towards the day and so very capable-looking, with his barrel body. Tenacious too, he was a mechanic but when they said mechanic they really meant a type of engineer. He never quantified all the machines he could build and repair—although the kids had all seen components he brought home to work on, and could make educated guesses.

He didn't offer this information up and they didn't ask and believed he was a decent man. For years, April had watched him and wondered if he carried any shame or guilt about putting working weapons in the hands of men with all sorts of agendas. She still hadn't come to an opinion on that yet. He didn't speak about it, basically ignored it, and that suppression made him stiffer and halting, April thought. Although it didn't define him, his body wasn't going to let him forget it. In truth, her own views on her dad weren't settled either, and so while she didn't feel Ben's animosity towards him, she didn't quite trust him either.

Their dad had favoured Nic with her clear work ethic and enthusiasm for learning, and she would spend Sundays with him repairing old machines or tools, and him letting her because his son was gone already and had never tolerated any interaction that would have involved their father giving guidance.

When the girls left after school, he'd largely absented himself as he watched his kids make an arse of living—getting fired, kicked out of this place, going to opposite ends of the country to hide the fact they were failing. Still, when he was in touch he couldn't quite stop himself from letting them each know what he thought of them.

April remembered getting drunk with Ben and convincing him that he should not join the military, no matter what their dad might have said. She worried what witnessing such violence would have done to Ben, much less perpetrating it. Some constitutions could take it, but not Ben's. 'And plus,' she'd said, 'look at Dad, is that what you want to be?'

Over the past few years, her dad was here again, tentatively, different when he was in the north on visits and then this spring he'd moved up here on a whim, he'd said, after seeing Star. April wondered if he'd become lonely and isolated and had just enough self-awareness to do something about it. Anyway, he'd stayed and they were all trying to adjust. But April didn't go overboard, kept up her guard, because he still had an edge to him.

The path cut up again and away. Beneath her skin were

the decisions made last night with Col, on the dance floor, on the porch, in her bed, and in the weeks and months before in the slow build of curiosity and trust and lust. A slow build and surer for it. April felt it so clearly, how she was newly bound and unwound and unwrapped by Col and somehow totally different and yet it was all totally familiar too—equalising—and the staid, fearful world she'd known had no purchase here. Happiness in flight at the corners of her mouth, in her toes, along her eyelids. In her breath. Joy. Stillness. Sureness.

Up and over the brow of the hill she stood amidst two clusters of abandoned crofts, with tufted lines of purple moor grass revealing where they'd runrigged the fields. When she lifted her head, magnificent views to the mountains of the north opened up. Were the people who lived here able to know this beauty amidst their back-breaking work? As hard as she worked now, she knew she had it easy. The sun's heat building, April headed back down to her own small cottage by a different path, one that led her directly home.

Finn woke and climbed down off his bed and up into the big bed next door. His mum and dad were pressed together in a hug in sleep, like he'd seen Star fall asleep on his mum, except Mum and Dad were nearly the same size. They didn't move to make space for him even when he scootched in close. Coughed. They'd laugh more during the day if they slept a bit more so he sat and read for what felt like forever. He turned the page, leaning over, poking one arm and then another. *Pssst. Pssst.* Eventually his dad unhinged himself from the unit they'd made and let Finn find a place within their bodies.

'Only if you sleep for awhile, you wee fisher.'

Finn nodded.

When he woke he was alone. His sister was in her cradle. She was pretty like a baby bird. He put his lips together and made a kissing noise that his dad sometimes made when they were walking outside. He said it called the birds to him but none ever came because of the call. 'Ppppp. Pppppp.' He whispered to her like his dad did.

'My wee Star. Wee Star.'

Reaching out, he rocked his sister where she lay. Back and forth. Back and forth. She was still and quiet until she rolled and rolled back and her gurning rose and twisted through the house.

'All safe,' Finn said. 'Wrapped up tight.'

She rolled up to the edge of the basket. Rolled through the middle and up the other side, kissing the edge of the basket.

Across Up Up Across. Up Up Up Up over the lip of the cot and she was gone.

His mum had swept his sister up into her arms.

'Whoopsie daisy.'

The girl bundled safe in her arms, she turned to him, her boy.

'Your dad is making pancakes, Finn, if you want to help.'

Guiding him off the bed, she took his hand, unlocked the magic gate and went down the stairs first. He followed all by himself.

'Today we're going to see April!

'And Ben!'

'Ben will come in a few days, but we'll see Aunt Grace.'

'And Grandpa! And April will take me to the water and to the broken house!'

And he'd walk through the woods leading the way because he was good at that. If it got dark he'd lead the way because he was bright inside, and they needed him to show them how to do it.

Nic watched Charlie make pancakes with Finn. He'd grown a bit wider around the waist. It suited him; Nic liked it. More to hold onto, more give in the thinning times.

Star's eyes followed Charlie whenever he was near. Nic

wondered if it was the tone of his voice she responded to, for he talked into the air, adding his notes to the world of sound of the house—amidst sleep, the buzz of the hot water tank, the crackling of the fire. Would it be the same among the sounds of the boat, the calling fulmar, the water, the drinking passengers? He was sweet as he swore quietly when he made a mess of the dishes or he stubbed a toe. He never quite seemed to know where his body was, where the furniture was.

'Did you move that table again?' he laughed at Nic.

'Yes, just for you,' she replied.

And sometimes she'd been tempted to do just that, but it wasn't necessary because he bumped, stubbed and banged regardless of anyone's actions. She thought of the quiet word he dropped into the space around him, just for her—beauty, gorgeous, hen— and a touch he bestowed, or a kiss. He didn't hover or impose or demand attention. He didn't need her affirmation or validation, neither did he need to take up that space unnecessarily. When it was quiet, when they needed quiet, like when fighting, or getting a child to sleep, his silence was full and at ease.

Nic sat with her feet up on a crate to give her back a break as she fed Star. Charlie and Finn were having fun making a mess. They could all leave early today, this morning, but they were lingering. The sun looked prepared to stick around and her garden beckoned.

'Want to go to the Summer Isles with your nursery class, wee fisher?' Nic asked her son.

Charlie looked at her with surprise and also a bit of pleasure. Rare were the days they had together on the croft.

Finn jumped up and down, and took a bite of the pancakes he held in his hand. 'Dad is letting me test the first one,' is what he'd said.

And now their son's feet danced and leapt and his voice was full of song and laughter.

Yes, Nic thought. Let us all take a rare day to ourselves.

Sonny was wide awake and had cramp in his leg from his position on the couch, but he stayed, stilled by his thoughts.

He and Viv had both been so foolish. All those years abroad, his job, how they'd fight and then move and the sex would be fantastic, like pressing restart on the whole thing. Sometimes that'd last for months: second and third and fourth honeymoons.

Viv was beautiful, of course.

But that didn't matter once she'd hit Ben and he'd hit back; or he'd hit her and she'd hit back. It didn't matter. It was

out of control and unacceptable and when she didn't talk about it that night it was her silence that was ugly. There was violence all around them, and their house had to be free of it.

She stood looking out at the street, a faint bruise rising on her cheek. Her breath was sour like she'd been drinking. In the afternoon.

'You need to do better with the kids,' Sonny said.

Nothing shifted in her, still there looking out the window. Nothing.

That's what they'd become. A shrugged, resentful silence. He wanted her to fight him in that intimate and political way they used to fight. So she'd take responsibility and throw some back at him too. To bring up how shitty this life was, how it was misogynistic of him to think he could take them anywhere in the world without consulting her, that he could tell her how to mother. That he needed to have a firmer hand with his son, teach him how to be a better man. What would that look like, Sonny wondered. How he should be doing anything but what he was doing, which was dragging his family around the world. He didn't have the power or right to order her to do anything.

She didn't do any of that and she didn't look at him but said, calmly, 'I know that, Sonny.'

Such a simple statement, but it wasn't hesitation or doubt

or a commitment. This was her way of pushing back, today. There was something detached about her, something he wanted to reach, to anger.

'I want you to leave.'

Sonny surprised himself by saying it. He'd been feeling it for so long it'd formed into words he didn't even have a chance to censor. The words were so easy to say now that he knew. He just knew there and then. Again, nothing happened except she poured herself more coffee, finishing the pot.

'I'll take that into consideration,' she said, eventually. She showered and put her packed bag by the door. The kids were in bed. She went in and kissed each of the girls, who didn't stir from their dreams. Ben's light was still on, despite his curfew, and she walked past, paused, but didn't knock or go in.

'Tell them whatever you need to,' she'd said to Sonny.

Sonny got up, put on trousers and made a move to get breakfast. The house was tidy because there was no one to mess it up. No one around to pick up after.

Ben's bag was light, as he'd packed in such a hurry, and the granite city was dead quiet as he walked. On other nights he'd make his

way through the grey graveyards, kicking aside grass or picking at the moss to read the inscriptions underneath. To find the skull and crossbones of the plague. He'd let his thoughts circle to his mum, dad, Sonia. Nothing good ever came of that habit. So he was trying to break it. His eye twitched and he put a hand over it to calm it. Today Ben found a bench that looked out over the water. He sat with himself and thought about picking up the fiddle like they did at New Year's and being rusty as hell, but giving it a go, as April did with the mandolin—those childhood music lessons were a distant memory and only vaguely of use; of dancing with Finn; telling dirty jokes with Grace. For some reason he envisioned Nic hugging him and him burying his face in her shoulder and crying. And her pressing her hands to his back, not letting go and saying, 'You're free, Ben. You've done it. It's messy, but I'm so proud.'

Grace took a cold shower first thing to wake herself up. She'd slept in, well past six, and there was so much to do today. On went an old pair of jeans, which were a bit tight, but she didn't let it play on her. The kids were coming today. She had cleaned the kitchen last night and its spotless counters and sink galvanised her this morning. A neat notice that the bakery would be closed for a full week was pinned on the bakery door and on her website. What a cheek in the middle of summer.

She went to the dresser for an old cookbook. The dresser was a muckle thing, apparently handmade by some nameless carpenter from Beauly. All the edges were straight and without ornament, almost Quaker-ish. It was full of books, games and sentimental keepsakes of people both living and dead.

She had an uncle who died at thirty-three, after stubbing his toe on a rusty nail (she had the nail). Her cousin died of meningitis at sixteen and she had a lock of her hair. Her mum had been thirty-two and her dad dropped dead at fifty-four of an aneurism after getting clean bills of health for years, and she had both their wedding rings. Hers and Viv's family didn't usually die of anything prolonged or profound. They dropped dead in a field after a day of farming, or on a hillside after a day of hunting, or mid-sentence, or from a bad case of the flu and there was rarely a thing any medical intervention could have done.

But Grace desperately wanted to grow old. She was living a life here and wanted to remember it all. The scar on her foot came from cutting it on coral in Hawaii, when cheffing for a prince on his yacht and diving off the back of the boat with his lovely bi-curious daughter to snorkel on Molokini. Loads of cuts on her hands from off-days or distracted preparation in the kitchen. Her frozen shoulder came from carrying too much up to base camp outside Nepal, as far as she would go, amidst the trampled ground and majestic peaks, to impress a sporty girl named Crystal who wouldn't make it to the top either. Grace told stories of her travels at parties to entertain and sometimes to smooth over awkward moments—so many of those in this family who were painfully earnest, resentful and carried the weight of their world as if it were the weight of the whole world.

For years Grace had wanted to say to those kids, and to Sonny too, that sometimes past things can feel very much present and, despite your efforts, they haunt you. They'd haunted Viv—things they didn't know, things Grace knew only partially—and so Grace could see how they haunted all of them too. It wasn't a quiet haunt either, but a loud one, a varied one, a clever one, and every time you thought you'd built resilience or restraint, every time you thought you'd shone light in all the corners, it snuck up from behind and cast doubts or threats right into the most sensitive bit of your spine. She'd started to think of it as an emotional legacy and she wondered what you could do to change it and make resilience the inheritance. She wondered if that's what she had done without thinking. She understood that she was lucky enough to have that relationship to the world.

Grace touched Suzie's knitting needles, which were crossed and resting on one of the shelves, and her hand brushed the old music box she'd not listened to in years and she edged it forward so she could wind it later and play it for everyone. Then she tucked her mum's cookbook under her arm and walked to the kitchen. Opening the book to the page she wanted, she leaned down, her waistband digging into her belly as she took out her biggest bowl to make today's bread. A dream accompanied her as she moved, so too did a resolve she didn't intend and couldn't quite read. She'd wait until Finn was here to make the fairy cakes and he could eat as much of the frosting as he'd like.

CHAPTER 9

Tilt

Nic drove down from Skye and Ben over from Aberdeen and they met in the car park further south and west. A path the other side of the road would give them access to Glen Tilt.

At 8am the place was already almost full. About fifteen cyclists were checking their bikes, stuffing their walking poles down the sides of their rucksacks, fitting their helmets onto their heads. They'd be riding up the Glen as far as the road would take them, off-road for a wee bit and then walk the most direct route up Beinn Mheadhonach. They faffed for ages as Nic and Ben made their own preparations, pulling on their boots and trying to decide about what clothing to bring. They didn't talk much; packing for hikes was something they were each proficient at.

'I've got my two-man tent,' Ben said. 'It'll be tight but should do us.'

'I might sleep out, depending,' Nic said, looking skyward.

Ben looked up at the blue outlining the still-bare branches of the trees. 'Yeah, you're right. We might be alright.'

'Go lighter.'

Ben nodded and checked the weather on his phone, felt his pack, thinking through what warmth and protection he had, and left the tent in the car. But he re-packed his fleece.

When they were little, their mum would lay everything they needed for a walk out on a bench or a counter or a table, depending on where they were living and staying. She'd have a pile each for Ben, Nic and April. The girls, when this started, were only toddlers, with tiny little packs, but she showed them, once, how to pack the heavier things—a book or an apple—at the bottom of the bag and then pack the lighter things around them so the pack sat comfortably on their back when they put it on.

'Or,' she'd say, 'you can find what you like best.'

April tried on her pack, paraded herself around the room and opened it up, took everything out and tried again. And again. Ben and Nic watched their mother pack her bag and imitated her, making small adjustments. They believed they always carried everything they needed themselves, but she had a huge pack with most of the food and extra clothes, the maps, the compass, the first aid kit. A real knife.

Dad would usually be working, but when he wasn't he'd join them, but their mum would organise the day and the things and he'd carry his own pack.

As they got older their mum did less preparation, simply shouting, 'Get yourselves ready,' except for the times she had one of her wobblies and she'd do nothing at all for any living creature, no matter how you asked. In the good times, they'd have discussed where they were going, how long the walk would be, and the kids would organise themselves. April always complained and resisted, but they all ignored her. She'd shut up at some point on the walk and love it. She'd tell the story of loving each and every walk and never talk about the hours or even days of complaining she'd do beforehand. Their mum would bring cake wrapped up in wax paper for a pre-walk snack, which usually got them through the worst of April's initial grump.

Their mum never quoted the Scouts' motto, *Be prepared*, but that's what she taught them back then. As soon as they could hold a knife, they buttered their own bread and spread their own jam. She taught them to tell the time so they could get themselves to school promptly, without waking her. They washed dishes standing on a stool, drying too, and then Nic would climb onto the counter to put the glasses and mugs away once dried. Soon they were making their own breakfasts and packing their own lunches for school and even learned how to make coffee for their parents who would be up and outdoors taking care of whatever else needed taken care of.

When they had shown themselves to be responsible handling sharp objects, their mum bought them each a small Swiss army knife. Ben first and then Nic and then April. When she handed it to April she said, 'Remember I can take this away from you at any time.' And more than once it was put on a high shelf for a rest as April showed a lack of the restraint and judgement befitting a Swiss army knife owner. When they started to go out for short walks on their own, they each got matching watches with unbreakable faces, 'so you know how long you've been walking,' and a compass, 'so you know in what direction.'

The last walk Ben remembered them taking as a family was up onto the plateau in the Cairngorms when he was thirteen, a few months before their mum left. No one was talking to anyone. He'd been given a warning about his bad marks at school and she was furious with him and strode off ahead, or sat to the side when they ate lunch, and didn't engage. It was complicated. The love, the anger, the impatience. He found, deep down, especially when he noticed her red eyes and the balled tissue in her hand, that he felt for her too, but this sympathy somehow only gave breath to his resentment. This was a walk where no one was happy and nothing was resolved.

Nic snapped a finger in front of his face. 'Hey, Ben,' and suddenly all the cyclist-walkers got on their bikes and tottered to the entrance of the car park, swithering about which way to go, and a woman among them shouted, 'Left. Left!' And off they all rode, to the left.

'We go to the right,' Nic said, hoisting up her bag and shoving the map into the netting at the front of his rucksack. 'Going up the estate road looks like the better route. We could cross the bridge and go up the other side but you're farther up the hill away from the river. The estate road hugs the water all the way to Marble Lodge.'

'Agreed.'

They started off on the well-maintained road, each taking the time to get into the walking. The road was compacted and easy to get a stride into and would roughen up a bit a few miles in and then again further up Glen Tilt at Marble Lodge. They planned to get to Forest Lodge by evening, camp, and follow the hills and ridges back. At the start, the path climbed quietly and slowly but not that high as the river cut its course through the glen. The river looked to be running at an average pace, although signs of last week's flood scarred the banks, which were cut anew in some places with the roots of trees exposed. A deer with its leg caught in the branch of a tree hung upside down where it had been swept down the hill by rain and mud. It might have survived had it landed legs first into the water. As it was, rising, rushing waters had submerged it up to its shoulders.

It was still cool in the woods at the start and they didn't talk much, only occasionally making observations about trees, plants and birds. Ben had seen peregrines mobbing an eagle here on a school trip years ago, the year he'd lived in Glasgow, and he remembered this glen fondly. It'd been Ben who'd suggested this walk.

Nic had a good stride, easy relaxed shoulders like their father's, and when she realised she'd forgotten her flask of hot coffee, and the car was an hour back, she tossed her hands above her head grinning with a self-admonishing tone, 'Really Nic? Really?'

It was a gesture that was full of her life and humour, and yet it reminded him of an action his dad had made during arguments when he'd chosen to de-escalate them. His dad's often serious face would soften, and he'd laugh, his right arm bending at the elbow and tapping twice at his heart. An unconscious confirmation of love.

She turned back to him and said, 'You think we'll see an eagle? Or a peregrine?'

He smiled and shrugged, had hopes. When she turned back to her walking, their strides nearly matched and the walking was easy as they came up to the end of the trees and entered the bright early spring glen. His sister started singing and he joined in, giving his chest a small tap, echoing the fluttering beat of his heart on the rise.

The path followed open moorland most of the way and offered no shelter from the day's sun. Ben put on his baseball cap. They walked until six or seven, when they found a good spot. They had seen the dead deer, loads of small birds, a mountain hare, a herd of deer, sand martins and a bird of prey they debated.

'It's a buzzard,' said Nic.

'No, a juv eagle,' said Ben, 'it's the glide.'

'Nope. Not convinced.'

When they stopped, Nic built an almost fierce fire, which was good because the temperature dropped with the clear sky. Ben boiled new salad potatoes and fried some steaks. They sat on the flat boulders they'd dragged to the fire pit.

'The rigs paying you well then, fancy pants?'

'Enough' he said and handed her an imported beer. 'Got me a flask of single malt in here too. What did you bring to the party?'

She got up and kissed his cheek and ruffled his hair. His knife was rusted and two of the elements wouldn't open, while another was about to fall off. Nic sat and fixed it while he cooked.

'How has it been working for the great Caledonian MacBrayne? How were the sailings over the winter?' Ben asked.

'The usual. Every few weeks it's blowing a gale at the wrong tide level and that's us scuppered at one port or the other. But if Charlie and the guys are on the boat, we all make do.'

'Charlie?'

Nic blushed. 'Yeah, well, he's part of the crew. Wants to be captain.'

'What a job.'

'Right? I hate parking a car, can't even think about how I'd bollock up parking a ferry.'

She exhaled in a way Ben couldn't quite read. Excited? Undecided? Afraid how much she might want this Charlie?

'The cafeteria is easier. It's mostly boring, full of the normal people filling time on the journey. I work the shop sometimes too—tourists, buying memorabilia. That, I totally understand. The mugs, postcards, chocolate bars and even the calendars. But. Nearly every trip I get people, locals—Scots, Islanders—shaking the CalMac calendar at me, complaining there aren't enough photographs of actual ferries on the calendar. What would make a person complain about that?'

'Nerds,' Ben said, as he touched the rim of his CalMac baseball cap. 'But seriously, they really should have more pictures of the boats on the calendars, they really should.'

Nic laughed. 'I didn't stick it out through three whole months of uni simply to get a job where I have to be the recipient of such complaints.'

'You're right. You failed to stick it out for the other three years and nine months you'd have needed to get a decent job.'

She threw a beer bottle cap at him.

'Instead you're *tinkering*,' Ben said, pointing to his Swiss army knife that Nic still had a hold of, as well as the now repaired zipper of his backpack, which she'd fixed while just sitting here waiting for her dinner to be ready.

Dad's word and they both knew it.

'Yes, I am 22, without a degree, and someone who likes to tinker. It means I'm resourceful and I recycle. What's wrong with that? I can fix your zipper or your penknife. Hire me.'

'Some guys might like the zipper part.'

'Bugger off.'

'Okay okay,' Ben held up his hands. 'What do you want to do?'

She flipped his knife open and closed, testing each tool and implement. 'I want to build and repair things.' She told him about how she'd loved apprenticing with Donald out on Uist until he had his heart attack and his creepy brother took over and how, now, on the ferry between shifts at port the guys would let her help them down in the engine room, and she had a knack for seeing the whole of a system and understanding how to make the component parts work. If she thought back on it all, there really wasn't an appliance or a domestic object that she hadn't taken apart and put back together again, or at least attempted to. 'Remember how Dad would bring home archaic or strange machines from boot sales or from estate sales where most of it was rubbish?'

'And he'd try to get us all to help him fix them.'

'You in particular, Ben.'

It wasn't how Ben remembered it. He remembered Nic and their dad hunched over some object, talking, trying things out. A unit.

'You were always out playing football.'

'And April had no time for it.'

'So it was just me and Dad for all those Saturdays. I think I have these fugitive memories of all those objects and all the actions we took to fix them lodged in the circuits of my brain like blueprints.' She moved her hands like their dad did and talked about how objects had certain weights to them, a certain balance and how she understood, often by touch, the resistance of a gear or wheel with the turn of the handle and what angles made all these small things do their jobs. 'So I love all that and wonder what I could do if I had a workshop. But,' she looked at Ben and everything about her vulnerable, 'what I really want to do is make babies. With Charlie.'

He laughed and opened his arms, beer spilling out of the bottle he'd tipped in the exuberance of the gesture. 'Babies! With some guy your big brother has never met. Is that allowed?'

Her blush burned through every inch of skin he could see. And he grinned. He should have seen it before, how she'd totally come into her own.

'You should do that.'

'What? Do what?'

'Start with the babies.'

'I've heard they ruin all the rest of it.'

He shook his head. 'Maybe. But maybe the babies will make it all possible.' He tapped his fingers against his bottle of beer. If Nic could do that, he could quit the rigs, try to convince Sonia he's the man for her, he could teach kids maths or set himself up as a gardener. According to her the rigs made him rude and grumpy. 'It's your anger,' she'd said, when she moved out last week. The unpredictability of it. The fierceness. She'd never been afraid of him, more afraid for him. 'This is big,' she'd said, placing an open hand over his heart. 'This is stubborn,' she said, keeping it there. She said she'd tried to help but it hadn't seemed to change anything. Although they'd talked since, she said she wouldn't come back until he'd sorted himself.

'Bugger,' said Nic, running her hand across the back of her knee to find the source of a nascent itch. 'The little bastard.' Then she was rummaging through her bag while Ben waited. She pulled out the tweezers, took off her walking trousers and with a careful clamp and gentle twisting pulled out a tick that had lodged itself into the warm, safe spot behind her knee. 'The little bugger.'

'It'll not have had time to do any damage.'

She hiked her trousers back up, 'They're disgusting.'

'April would be proud. For all her complaining, that girl can always get rid of unwanted shit. Boyfriends, ticks, leeches.'

'Remember those leeches?'

'Yes,' Ben said, giving a small shudder.

Ben had been twelve or thirteen, maybe, and the girls nine. They'd been swimming in a freshwater lake somewhere. April was building sandcastles while Nic and Ben played shark in the shallows. They weren't alone in the water, and each of them had half a dozen leeches clamped onto their legs and torsos by the time they got out. Ben was calm, but Nic totally freaked out. Her sister tried to talk her down.

'It's okay, it's okay. I know what to do.'

But Nic wouldn't calm down.

'Stop it Nic, or I'll slap you.' April shook her a little bit with a hand firmly gripping each of her bare arms, still wet from the water. April's hands were a bit sandy, but she wiped them fast and hard off her thighs to clean them. 'Sit.'

Nic sat down and April sat down beside her and picked off the leeches one by one, taking a firm grip of each, giving a quick tug, and then tossing them into the grassy sand. 'One, two, three,' she counted. 'Another one bites the dust.' And then she said, laying a hand on Nic's shoulder, 'All done.'

She turned to her brother who was jumping from one foot to another, twisting to see all the creatures attached to his legs, almost afraid to check beneath in his swimsuit.

'And now you.' Ben stood while she did the same to him. They all checked under their swimsuits. Ben had a tiny one, a baby, right on his willy.

'Can you?' he asked April. She nodded and it was done in a flash.

Each leech left a bloody kiss behind; small, but a mark of their bravery.

Ben and Nic laughed as if it was all just another thing that happened all the time. April had gotten up and walked to the edge of the beach; they heard her heaving up her guts.

'Did you hear that April got fired from that bar down in Glasgow?'

'I sure did.'

'How do you get fired from a pub like that?'

'But that's April. She gets bored and so sticks her finger in that socket and lets the failure shock through her.'

'Were punches thrown?'

'You know, maybe the usual. What us Avenses seem to encourage,' Nic said, and they both knew well enough. 'There was a proper brawl. She was in a right state. The pub too. I think they're trying to hold her accountable for the damages.'

'Drinking on the job, eh?'

'I couldn't possibly say. But she was retching for a full day after, all the way up on the bus.'

'Her fellow passengers must have loved her.'

'Then she took to her bed for almost a week.'

'At Grace's?

'Yes. The two have been going head to head since. "That girl does nothing by halves," Grace said to me. I reminded her it'd only been ten days, and she'd been laid up sick for seven of those. "That's ten days too many," she said.'

They laughed, and when they looked up, night had fallen.

There was a nearly full moon and bright stars. Unrolling their sleeping bags on either side of the fire they kept it stoked as they told stories back and forth, sometimes falling into silence as they think about their own things, and then they stopped feeding the fire and let sleep arrive.

Ben lay on his back and watched the sky. Sleep was brief. His dreams, realistic. He woke and continued to watch the sky. He carried the same feeling whether awake or asleep.

Listening to his sister laughing in her sleep, he tried not to be jealous, and finally slept dreamlessly until the birds singing at first light woke him.

The next day they shared beans, sausages, toast and coffee. They crossed the river and headed up for a day of tougher walking. They worked harder and talked less. Ben saw his peregrine. He fist-pumped the air. Yes.

The walking took them both over. They must be thinking things, important things on this walk, but in amicable silence neither of them talked about them on this second day. The smell of sun on the earth rose up to greet them as they kicked up dust. The sound of spring and sometimes a burn or the river when they descended into a corrie before heading back up to a ridge and down to their cars.

'What a trip.'

'Exactly.'

'We should do this every year.'

'Deal. Every year.'

Ben lingered and was taking his time putting things in the boot of his car. He wanted to tell Nic about the flying, about how Sonia had broken up with him, and what she'd said about him, and about how he knew nothing about how to be happy. A few flies hung around the sweat on his neck and at the baseline of his hair. He swiped at them but they didn't make him move any more quickly.

Nic whipped off her socks and put them in her boots.

'Ta da!' She brandished a pair of sandals. 'Heaven. After a long walk, nothing beats a pair of sandals.'

'Ta da!' Ben mimicked her and held up his own. But he still had both boots on and only then put one foot up on his bumper to unlace the first one.

'Fish and chips?' Ben suggested. 'There's a hotel in Blair Atholl and it didn't look too scary.'

'Yeah, sure.' Nic closed her boot and opened her door, sliding her water bottle into the side-well. She looked to the road and to the sun.

Ben's eyes followed her gaze. 'Okay. Okay. I get it. You want to hit the road. Get back to that boy of yours.'

'No, no. Let's go for dinner.'

'No way. I understand. I'm just a brother. Go get your butt back to your man.'

Nic blushed. From toes to ears. Blushed like it was an adrenalin surge, and it only grew stronger as she came up to Ben and had him in a hug before he'd even finished speaking. 'Never second, Ben. Never. This has been brilliant. The best walk I've had in ages. It's been great to see you. It's been too long.'

Ben nodded, extracted himself and tried to shake off the slowness he felt. He removed one boot then the other. Nic standing there. Her hand on his back. Sandals on. She stood on tiptoes and kissed his cheek.

'I'll see you soon, right.'

'You bet, sis.'

CHAPTER 10

The sun was already bright and Sonny carried a bold hope that each day would be long and a sure sort of exquisite. With the basic chores done, the rented house was clean enough and easy to leave.

He climbed onto the used, rather rusted bike he'd picked up last month at a car boot sale. The wheels turned and the tyres kept the air once he gave them a bit of attention. He wore shorts and a T-shirt even as the goose pimples rose on his arms and legs. Soon enough, the effort of the hills would tame them. He turned the bike uphill on the road and took off at a relaxed pace as he'd done nearly every morning since March. Choosing different roads, Sonny flirted with the disorientation, the undulating, inconsistent hills of all shapes and sizes, that met like puzzle pieces conjured so quickly, and he'd ride on, eventually coming across a familiar road or path, and find his way back. He was piecing this place together, here and now, re-creating memories that for years he'd been afraid to forge, not only here but in any place. Around the corner, another view was framed by the slant of a hill, the zig-zagged treeline and the gentle light of this time of day. His keen eyes scanned hawk-like for *For Sale* signs, a small plot, anything he could do something with.

He'd grown up twenty-seven miles to the northeast, in another rural collocation of houses—an only child, much loved, much judged. His parents had hated Viv for reasons they wouldn't voice, and Sonny had chosen her over them, as you do when you're young. Viv and Grace's mother was already dead, and her dad and stepmother were good-enough people, but not keen on him either, and so it was easy for them both to leave.

The summers here, they were part of it too. The summers before the kids, only two or three of those, had been raucous. With naked swims in the loch and too much drink. Him, Viv, Grace and whoever she'd invited over for the summer. Much of this was time spent avoiding his parents who were still alive and still disapproving of the marriage, and trying not to wake Viv and Grace's stepmother Suzie, who was asleep upstairs, already unwell, they all now know, but at the time they all thought she was just older and a bit tired. His parents never did soften but Sonny would visit them alone, although he insisted on showing them photos of the wedding and of each of the kids as they arrived. It was with some sadness that his parents never met his kids. An absence on both sides. Perhaps he carried those feelings here too. And a few summers in, when he returned to the cottage after seeing his folks, Grace handed him a beer.

'Families,' she said. 'They're a pain in the arse.'

'I hear you, sister.'

And he watched that word settle in with her as an obvious, shared pleasure.

Sonny coasted downhill and around a curve and started the climb up on the other side that'd take him to the house. Viv's question looped: *Are you all at Grace's, like usual?* Viv. Here. The possibility of it winded him, punched his lungs.

Handling Viv all those years had depleted him. She'd hated his job and called him complicit. But he wasn't. He was taking care of his family. Her outrage was a coil in her belly, burning red-hot, and she'd made futile, dangerous attempts to change the world that only served to unsettle them all. He wanted to tell his son and daughters how sometimes everyday things can undo a person. How sometimes small, regular responsibilities are overwhelming and sometimes there's no reason for how you feel. Despite his job, Sonny viewed himself as the pacifist; it was Viv who was the pugilist. That's where his kids got it from. And witnessing it had made it hardwired. How do you untangle that?

When Viv left them, Sonny had packed up the kids and moved them to a small two-bedroom flat in Glasgow. Sonny took one bedroom, the girls the other, and Ben slept on the sofa bed in the sitting room, which he loved because he had unmonitored access to the telly and then hated because he had no privacy whatsoever, and Sonny encouraged him to make his bed by 7am sharp, each morning. They were rocky times. These times here were only moderately less so.

His shirt stuck to his back from the final climb up to the house and Sonny put his feet on the ground and looked out. The pleasure and comfort he felt at living here shocked him just a little. He leaned the bike against the back of the house, changed his clothes, made a travel mug of tea and headed out to the car to pick up April.

April showered and put on her usual pub attire—jeans and a T-shirt. She brought a light waterproof jacket just in case, but she felt the day would go the other way—towards heat and closeness. Like last night.

Her dad had mentioned Viv in an off-handed sort of way when she'd called him this morning and the thought of Viv agitated her but she let it play around a bit, and it calmed. It was just being in this place, getting together, that made her dad nostalgic for something that never was.

As she got to the road, her dad pulled into the passing place, reached over and opened the passenger door.

'Morning, April.'

'Morning, Dad.' She leaned in and gave him an awkward kiss on the cheek.

That was all the settling in he needed and he set off. The day was a pretty one but the silence felt fraught. April made a start.

'Your favourite sister-in-law asked me to ask you if you could take a look at her car.'

Grace owned a second-hand 4×4 that had never run right. She'd burned through the engine once and said it was about to go again.

'I'll not be able to find anything wrong. It's broken because she rides the clutch.'

It's a long-standing disagreement and Grace had said, more than once, 'I'll ride that know-it-all's fucking clutch.' The two of them had always butted heads but created a relationship based on practical arrangements. And yet Grace's car too often sat in the lay-by on the road below her house and April wasn't convinced it'd take them where they needed to go in an emergency, so she hoped there were no emergencies. 'Please, Dad. She needs the car and is too proud to ask.'

'You mean stubborn, not proud.'

April shrugged, nodded.

'I'll have a look at it next week.'

'You sure you'll still be here?'

'I'm sure, I'll still be here,' he said, as if it was foolish for her to think otherwise.

'Will anyone else be here too?'

Sonny slowed for a curve and didn't accelerate after, gripping the wheel. 'What made you ask that?'

'A hunch. You've been cagey, and you mentioned Mum when we talked. You never talk about Mum.'

He nodded. 'Your mother emailed last night. She was wondering if we were all here. She was thinking of stopping by.'

'Stopping by? More like crash-landing in the middle of a party. You told her to piss off, right?'

'It's not my decision to make.'

'Of course it is. She contacted you. She wants to show up, set off fireworks and leave again. You can prevent it.'

'Give her some credit. She could have showed up unannounced. She was testing the waters.'

'Why didn't you tell her those waters were full of angry, abandoned sharks?'

Despite her wonderful night, despite the morning, red built up behind April's eyes, buzzing her lips into tightness.

'I was just passing on information.'

'So I can stress about it? You've never understood the power you have, Dad. Or the responsibility. She undid this family and you allowed her to.' She looked out the window. 'I get it though. We're adults and we need to make it right ourselves. We shouldn't be relying on you.'

'Maybe it'd be good for us all to try to make it right.' He started the car and pulled onto the road.

'Have you told Grace?'

'No.'

'Tell her.'

She looked out the window, consciously breathing. Her temper cooled. She could handle this. It would require them all being human together.

'I worry,' she said. 'About Ben in particular. But Nic's pretty pissed too.'

'And you?'

'I can take her or leave her. But I'd rather leave her. And it may never happen and so we can carry all this worry about a knock at the door that never comes. The threat of it.' April shook her hands and head free of it. Her dad put a hand on her shoulder.

'Exactly. So should I tell Nic and Ben?'

'My head hurts already. She does this to us.'

April's phone buzzed and she glanced down, then up to her dad. 'Nic and Charlie are having a slow start, something about Star not sleeping and Finn going on a trip with his nursery class. They might leave mid-afternoon.'

'Got it.' If he was angry or disappointed, she couldn't tell.

'Leave it for now and we'll be ready to firefight. Tell Grace,' she repeated because Grace kept a cool head around her sister. She realised her dad was heading for the pub. 'Actually, can you swing by the community hall so I can pick up my car?'

'If your car is there, how did you get home last night?' He tapped his finger on the steering wheel, raised an eyebrow, looked at her, trying to lighten the mood. 'Or, more importantly, who did you bring home last night?'

'Wouldn't you like to know?'

'Yes. Yes, I would very much like to know.'

And even as she was certain in ways she'd never been certain before, she didn't have the words for what Col was to her, what they were to each other. Plus, this was her dad, and he'd never exactly been someone she told anything. 'A wise woman never tells.'

'Even when she's getting a free lift?'

Her phone pinged. Another cluster of sibling-texts. 'Ben is on the bus. He gets in at noon and wants to know if I can collect him from the bus station.'

'His shift on the rig isn't over for two more days.'

'Well, he's back now. You can ask him why. I'll tell him to get a taxi to the pub, I'll feed him, and you come and get him around 2?'

His hands stiffened on the wheel but he kept his face relaxed. 'Of course. It's great he'll be here tonight.' Sonny pulled up alongside her car. There was a note under the windscreen wiper.

'From lover boy?'

'Something like that.' She opened the door, half in, half out. 'Thanks, Dad.'

'Invoice will be in the post,' he pointed to the odometer, then to his forehead, ascribing the miles travelled to memory and smiled. Next time she got in his car she expected to see her name in his little book.

April had grown fond of The Still, especially the unnatural quiet of the pub before it opened. There was comfort in the gleam of the bottles, clipped into place upside down for easy measures; the more expensive spirits tail-down, label righted, waiting to be tipped. The simple satisfaction of pulling a good pint. She'd started to think that asking the big questions messed you up. Find a place that wasn't horrible and build from there. Find someone like Col and everything else might just be bearable, might even become brilliant.

It was nothing like the local dive where she'd worked in Glasgow during her third year of uni, and perhaps she'd been drinking, screwing around and loafing—basically anything but studying—but she had punched a regular named Ian, and he'd punched her back and then some. What a wanker. The owner's only intervention was to make space for the brawl by pushing folks and tables out of the way. Seriously. April wasn't a fighter, not really, but those hands on her bum, brushing her breasts as she gathered empties. She'd fought with words first; all women learn to do that. But he'd grabbed her arm (she has photos of that ring of blue-purple-orange fingers) and gave her a right feel, *These types love this*, he'd said, making ape noises for his pals. His mates hooted, spurred him on. She'd swung her other arm, made contact, and then with no hesitation at all he let her have it. He beat his wife, she knew it then and knew it now. Such an easy familiarity with taunting and hitting women. She'd glimpsed the owner watching the fight, wiping the bar with a rag, his wife stood a few steps away out of his line of sight, unconsciously rubbing her cheek bone. The bar's cameras picked up the whole thing, but the news only showed the clip of April landing the first blow. Male violence was assumed, lauded; female violence was news.

She'd arrived at Grace's with a bruised jaw and defeated will. Ice bridled the road, the taxi from the bus station wagging its tale like a fin on the rural roads but making it to the bottom of Grace's drive. Grace came down with a sledge to meet her and help her with her bags. The cottage looked different. Grace had re-pointed the stones, put in new windows, given everything a once-over with paint, and it looked more lived-in, more settled into the ground. Not only was the house wind- and water-tight, it had become very much Grace's own. April could see that from a glance and she expected to follow Grace and the sledge up the small incline to the house. Instead, Grace handed her the rope.

'What do you think I am, your servant?'

And so it began. This was not going to be a beautiful friendship.

There was a new porch of a traditional sort, rectangular and robust. The front door opened into a vestibule laden with hooks and horsehair mats for wiping your boots on and a wooden rack to store them. Grace stood and pointed in various directions.

'Coat here. Scarf and hats here. Boots here. There's also a new utility room at the back door, if you prefer.'

'This is fine,' April said, but when she tried to enter, Grace told her to wait.

'Can't you see, there's only room for one of us in here at a time.'

Grace was moving relatively quickly but the air bit at April's neck and the back of her legs and she stomped with annoyance.

Stepping into the house, Grace nodded at April, 'It's all yours, Patience.'

'I don't want one of your nicknames.'

'Well you've got one. You need to have patience to live here as you're going to try mine. I can tell.'

Grace hadn't done any work to the loo that was on the ground floor, in the far corner. It had a tiny standing shower that was perfectly functional for a woman living on her own. April already knew that the pissy little drip from the shower would drive her around the bend. Upstairs, also untouched, two tiny bedrooms were crammed in under the eaves as though Grace and her low-expectation guests might be swallows or house martins tucked up tight in a nest. She had dilapidated outbuildings she never mentioned, which sat on messy land, beyond a neatly fenced-in garden, that she rented to a local farmer. April got into the habit of tending to the fence with Grace, painting the slats every year, as weathering demanded. The forging of a hesitant co-habitation was simply an extension of this, and as they did chores, or as they made dinner, they'd talk and sometimes sing as they went, usually caterwauling through common ballads where a woman is wronged and then dies by a man's hand, who has also been wronged and sometimes dies too.

That'd been 2012, six years already. She wasn't sorry about the punch-up or moving to Grace's but didn't want to have to do that again. And she'd learned too, so that by the time she found herself ruining her chances in her new job at the housing office in Inverness, she knew to make words do enough of her fighting for her. For those few statements, her boss sent her packing.

She'd gone back to doing odd jobs and then just before Christmas last year found herself here at The Still. April loved the challenge of the rowdy hours, the known quiet of calmer times. The sense of responsibility she had for making the space work. April was early today and she gave everything in the bar an extra once-over before helping Hannah prepare in the kitchen.

Col's job was all about water—finding sources of water, digging wells, re-routing flood waters—and Scotland was a challenging place to work. Everyone cared about water and even though it seemed abundant, politics and questions of ownership abounded. Today Col was up at Letters with a regular client trying to help with a landslide issue. Across the loch, Ullapool caught the morning sun. April was the type of woman Col should be dating, and last night she'd moved towards what they might be, not away. Nearly mid-morning, still early, but Col was alert, all senses firing. A few hours' work here and Col could make it down to Inverness for a late lunch at The Still. What a rush, these feelings for her. Etiquette went out the window in the face of this urgency. At the first opportunity, Col would go old school and phone her, even though it was still early, even though she was still at work, even though Col had no idea what they were to each other yet.

Nic gardened with Star sleeping in her car seat tucked up in a corner of the plot while Charlie took Finn down to the water for a while. What had started as a tiny, tentative walled garden two years before had somehow managed to thrive. Over the winter, Nic had made it bigger by moving the two internal walls further into the field, stone by stone (and carrying others from the edges of the fields to extend them). It was still a hesitant garden and in the vegetable patch there were many holes the size of Finn's keen hands. The yield would be average. Enough.

Nic looked up at Charlie who stood leaning on the wall, Finn with his chin on his dad's shoulder. 'Cup of tea, love?'

'Yes, please.' She stood and kissed Charlie. Then she kissed Finn too.

Charlie reached over and picked up Star in her seat. 'Take your time.'

An hour and then another passed and Nic hadn't noticed. When she heard Charlie load the kids into the car to take Finn to the pier where the boat would take them all to the Summer Isles, she stood, noticed the mug, which Charlie must have brought at some point, resting at the top of the wall. The tea had gone stone cold. She turned towards the house and Charlie tooted the horn. She waved. Finn blew her kisses through the open window, and she sent him kisses of her own.

Beyond the house, the workshop was finally watertight. Donald had sent a few friends with orders her way. They sent her long emails describing the tools they needed and saying how Donald recommended her work.

She read and re-read each email. She replied to each person, saying she didn't yet have a place or the equipment to make things yet, but would get back to them when she did. A few had offered different machines and she'd accepted. Charlie scratched his head at each new arrival, still wondering what she was going to do and, more importantly, when she'd get started.

A few days ago, Donald's wife Mhairi had asked about a tool she needed to do her weaving and Nic had been mulling it over. She had some ideas, but partial, nothing firm. Then, here, down amongst the runner beans, it was suddenly clear. She pushed back her hair, could feel the dirt she'd left behind on her forehead, but went out to the workshop where she'd set up a table and chair in the middle of the open space that would become something. She sketched it. Dated it. Put Mhairi's name at the top.

She'd been finding that this was how it worked for her: after days of not knowing what might be needed, the tool that would work for each task arrived to her fully formed as if out of the blue. Usually, like today, when she was doing something else. It'd been a joy the last few weeks that after years of this blank space where this thinking should be, suddenly, there were these things.

Nic headed back out onto the croft. Their croft, home.

Finn talked all the way to Achilitbuie. Charlie listened, nodded, asked questions, and hoped he could drop Finn off and get back to croft without waking Star.

At the pier, they saw all Finn's friends and the teacher waiting for him. Finn was trying to get his hands to unfasten the buckles that held him firm.

'Hold it fisher, I'm coming,' and Charlie freed his son who climbed down. Charlie squatted and offered his cheek and opened arms. His son leaned into them, kissed him, and then ran towards his friends. Squealing.

Charlie and the teacher exchanged waves and he got back into the car and headed home. Work had been intense. The day captain called him in and said he thought he'd be a good bet for the officer track. He could become a captain, he said; he saw that in him. He would support him in gaining his certificates. Charlie hadn't told Nic yet. It would mean studying in Glasgow and more time away from the croft and her and the kids. They'd talked about him working on the ferries in the long term. It'd be a hard life for them both. He thought about his dad's bad habits abroad with the merchant navy and knew he could and would do it better. But it was a different future than they had talked about, with him at sea almost half the year. The croft really would be her endeavour.

He turned onto the single-track road, and then onto the thinner track and then onto their drive. As he drove slowly around the final curve, the new building emerged, all ready for them to make something of it. For Nic to make something of it.

He'd noticed the concentration she had when she turned to things she loved and he was envious of it. He had it on the boat, sure, but not here, and it might worry him, if that continued. The croft was theirs, they shared it, she said, but his heart resisted the surrender. It wasn't his dream.

He'd come across some drawings she'd made and catalogues had started to arrive for the equipment she needed to get started. She'd been collecting clamps and other things, and often he'd come home and there'd would be a hand-me-down steel and wood bench set or metal working lathe sitting beside the wood lathe her father had given her, a used bandsaw and strange things Nic told him were a flux core welder and a die-grinder—it made the soldered joins smooth. People would come off the ferry and drop things off for her. He could have brought it up, he'd say to her, but she'd not told him, not asked for help. Her desk was full of drawings of strange, unique tools that were clear and intricate. Some of them had names written on them. He'd need to ask her about those. Was she already taking orders when it was clear they weren't ready to fill them?

Things were constantly changing and it was their job to be aware of that, shift them in directions they'd like to travel. Lifting Star from her seat, she woke. He shoogled her and rubbed his head into her belly. She couldn't yet grab his hair, but she would soon enough. But she liked the action and she calmed as he put her in the sling that bound her to him. He walked towards Nic and he planned to take her hand and they'd go for a walk. He'd tell her of the captain's praise, that he wanted to try, and he'd make sure they'd figure this next bit out together because that's certainly not how it had started out.

On the bus Ben nursed a builder's tea in a takeaway cup, listening to the forthright type of older woman sitting beside him who always seemed to seek him out on public transport. She was a primary school teacher with strong thoughts on education and play.

'Smart use of video games in learning is the way forward. That and good old-fashioned books. We need to take things in our hands, to hold them, actual objects. We need to face them directly for them to be real in this world,' she thumped her chest. 'Spur on those imaginations, non-linear thinking and something we can put our hands on and know through our own eyes, through what we can make our hands do.'

Her eyes glimmered. 'We need real people. And that's why I always sit beside someone on the bus, even if there are empty seats.'

Lucky me, Ben thought. He wished he had his car and was speeding along the backroads, perhaps, maybe taking the turns too fast, maybe letting go of the wheel, to see what that's like.

Not far after they left the station, Ben pretended to sleep. His companion, Pip, patted his shoulder and moved seats.

'I can take a hint,' she said. 'Have a good holiday with your family. Arnica helps with bruises,' she said as she pressed a small tube of cream into his hand.

As the landscape grew hillier, he realised he'd taken the slow bus and they'd be going up and over the pass at Tomintoul. It'd take forever to get to Inverness. But it was pretty. Lochnagar was near here and he and Nic had walked the hill, camped nearby, gone to the pub, talked all night. For a college dropout, she was ambitious. She was apprenticing with Donald, as a joiner in the Hebrides, and had plans to buy a croft and start her own business. Even back then he told her he was going to quit the rigs.

And somewhere in this remembering his pretend sleep became real, and he passed most of the miles of the trip this way, dreaming of driving and swimming and escape. He woke up not at all rested with sweat winding a way down his spine.

Ben peeled back the bandage and surveyed his arm. Sally had done a good job. There was no flourish, no statement that asserted it was the end, as if she too knew his weaknesses and that he may again, in the future, go back to the easy money of the rigs. The old scar, cut along the artery of the delicate part of his wrist, reminded him of what a small, ineffective cry he'd made when he was fifteen. He'd done it, realised it was stupid, called out and it was Nic who arrived, cleaned him up, covered for him with their dad. Dad had known the truth but he accepted the lie and didn't push either of his kids. Perhaps he'd thought it was enough that the siblings were in it together. As Ben remembered, there was a churn in his gut, the sluggishness of his head and his eyelids. Here his mouth went dry, his throat constricted and he couldn't speak if he tried. This was familiar, too, and he let himself drop off into another troubled sleep.

As they pulled into the bus depot, Pip was back and placed her cool hand on the heat of his arm. 'You talk when you sleep,' she said. 'How could they not love a beautiful, kind man like you?'

CHAPTER II

The Croft

Time can stretch and bend and shorten; for Nic, it was often lost.

The urges Charlie conjured in her dismayed Nic—part of her wanted to give him everything. Her knees buckled, her thighs ached, and her centre was sweet and sang and she wanted to hit an open palm to her head, shake her limbs. She often gave herself a good talking to.

Snap out of it. Get some sense Nic. You haven't worked so hard to lay it all down for a man.

Then Charlie grinned at her. Brought her a catch of fish that he'd grill over an open fire. And she'd lay him down or he'd lay her down and it'd hit her harder. It made her dizzy and the world shook and rattled her to the bone. It was addictive.

Down on one knee, in the middle of the restaurant on the ferry, a plate of fish and chips held aloft, Charlie proposed and Nic said yes, laughing, taking a chip and dipping it in mayonnaise. She took half and, after double dipping, gave the other half to Charlie. A round of applause from colleagues and passengers alike. She swooned and looked around to see if it was the boat on a swell. It was not. She slid her hand down his arm to his elbow and brought him to standing. He was solid like a wall in his overalls and his wind-styled hair. He was a walking talking contradiction: generosity and unmoveable will; kindness and stubbornness; love and, well, there was only love there.

The crowd took it as her demand for a kiss. Charlie lifted his arms into the air and succumbed, like he will as a groom when their families and friends knock forks against the champagne flutes. Someone accepted the plate of chips from Nic and Charlie kissed her and this thing swept over her: she would change her name, have babies, the whole shebang.

Over the next few days she fought that urge. She had to work hard to imagine her skeleton as her own, the blood through her body as her own, this sweet demand, her own. She tamed the stupidity. She would keep her name. They would wait to have kids. She would get some land and build the house. Well, she hadn't told him that last bit yet.

Although it'd be easy to think that Nic had been directionless since she dropped out of uni, this was not the case. She had dropped out and simply got to work. Nic had some money saved but not nearly enough. She'd searched and asked around and found a tiny croft for sale, which was less expensive but came with responsibilities. She couldn't really afford the land and she had no idea how she'd find what she would need to build the house. She didn't call her dad or Grace or April. She didn't ask Charlie. She called Ben and invited him up to the plot. He couldn't come up and was to her mind a wee bit cagey about the reason, but he didn't hold back on his enthusiasm for the idea. Instead right then and there he asked, 'How much do you need?'

She told him.

'I can't quite do that.'

'But I thought you were minted.'

'This gig isn't going to last forever.'

'Change afoot?'

'Not the time, sis. I'm running out the door.'

He made rustling noises and Nic knew avoidance when she heard it. She'd not push. There'd be time soon.

'I can do half of that. How much do you have?'

'Some.'

'You want what I got?'

Nic was thinking that it wasn't enough. She didn't say that. It was something. It was amazing. She'd see if she could make it work.

'Yes, but I'll have to see if I can get the rest or knock the price down. I'm not sure he really warmed to me. I'm not sure he took me seriously. His eyes kept look at me like I was just a girl. It's also going cheaper because they're looking for a local and because the land is a hard sell, hard to access, harder to make something of. I'm not even sure I qualify as a local.'

'You've been out that way nearly four years. You should be able to make a case. Plus, if he's treating you like a girl, just show him how much of a girl you are. Show him how much you want it, how hard you'll work, what a good neighbour you'll be. Nic, it sounds perfect. You'll let me visit right?'

'I'm going to put a hammer in your hand to help me get the place up and running.'

'You mean help both of you out, Charlie and you.'

'Yes, yes. That's what I mean. He's thrilled. But your agreement is with me. I'll pay you back,' she said.

'You better,' he laughed, 'with interest.'

Ben transferred the money by the end of the week. She typed up a payment plan and signed it and sent it to him. From that day on she called him The Shark. And when they were together and she shouted to him in greeting he'd open his arms super wide with that massive reach he had and clamp them down. Rauragh'd. And when she got closer he'd close his arms around her and hold her tight.

*

After Grace got off the phone with Nic she'd made plain scones. Quick to throw together, hers were always messy, barely brought together as a wet dough and slapped onto the baking sheet—rocky droppings that baked light and moist and broke apart and soaked up the melted butter so well. She baked them and, still warm, sliced two open, slathered them with butter and jam, and then put them in the tin with the rest of the unsliced scones. Within an hour of Nic's call, she was in the car with the tin lid flipped half open on the passenger seat to let the steam out, hoping she didn't meet any stupid people who forced her into an emergency stop. She met Nic at the end of the road, as directed.

'This will be something to see,' she said.

They walked the land together. As near to the property line as they could manage. Over heather and mounds of earth, there were ditches and slopes and lots of rocks.

'Pick some smaller ones up, it's never too early to start clearing the land.'

'It's not yours yet.'

Nic nodded and picked up a stone and put it in her pocket. And Grace found herself reaching down, picking them up too. She snapped two smooth stones together, fancying they might spark. A clear, resonating sound.

'Stonechat,' Nic said.

It was a statement of the sound, which was the origin of the bird's name too, and it also felt like a decision had been made and something had changed irrevocably. The stones made the sound again, smaller and quieter, like an echo or a confirmation, when Grace put them in the pocket of her cagoule.

'Where will the house go?'

'The planning docs allow for a croft house and an outbuilding.'

Nic headed directly out across the land to the highest point. She outlined the house, placing stones she had been gathering in the corners and adding a few more.

Grace stepped over the rock outline and stood inside the house. Looked out, as if at the window, 'Great view.'

Nic stood beside her.

Grace didn't play with the stones in her pocket or place her arm around the girl's shoulder as she wanted to, felt she needed. Her sister had abandoned her kids a long time ago and Sonny had made himself absent in different but equally effective ways. That's why Nic was asking her for money to support her dreams—because her parents had made themselves unavailable. Viv had been gone for forever; Sonny should know better but clearly didn't care. She could slap them both.

'And what else? How are you going to make it work?'

'We'll keep hens. Have a garden, maybe sell some of what we grow.'

They looked at the land; it looked mean and like it would take some work to tame it.

Grace nodded. 'Or? And?'

'I've not decided. I'm not good with cars like Dad. But I'm pretty good with machines, fixing things, and building. But builders are a ten a penny. I did a bit of metal work with Donald out on North Uist and I really liked that. I made some bespoke replacement parts for older tools or machines and even made a few new tools to do specific, awkward jobs, which I liked even more.'

Now Grace gave her niece a quick side-on hug standing there where a window might be. 'You have some work to do. Some decisions to make.'

'I love this place.' She looked out and they stayed quiet for a few minutes. 'And I love Charlie.' Her pause was a long one.

'But?' Grace prompts.

'I'm not sure I have the mettle to be good wife or a good crofter. I worry that by being his wife, I'll surrender something to him. It's such a high price. Grace, I'll come clean. I'm asking you because I've not told Charlie about this yet. It's mine. I need it to be mine. I'll share it, of course and it'll become ours, but it'll be mine first. I can't say why that's, essential but it is.'

Grace gathered her in fully then, in a gesture she'd never made with Nic or any of the kids before. Kissed the top of her head. And then pulled back. It was a quick action. Of love, but hesitant.

'I understand all that. Why do you think I'm single? I even glimpse a bit of what you're talking about and I run, hop on a plane/boat/the back of a motorcycle and am out of there. So, I'm in. I'd like to see what it's like when someone doesn't flinch. What I have is yours.'

They shook hands.

'Draw up that payment plan you're using with Ben and sign it. I'll hold you to it like nobody's business.'

'Absolutely.'

They stepped over the stones but left them on the ground and walked back to their cars. The car door was unlocked and Grace pulled out the tin and offered Nic a scone, placing the tin on the roof of Nic's car so she could take them back with her.

The women ate their scones looking out to sea where the gulls and kittiwakes swooped white against the blue of the water and the grey of the rock.

'You better get back to April before she tears your place apart.'

Grace laughed. 'Then she'd have no roof over her head.'

'You know that when she got fired and ended up back at yours she left a message on my phone. Just "Help. Me."'

'What did you do?

'I waited three days and texted her back. "Grow. Up."'

'And?'

'And she's not really been back in touch since.'

'I'm not worried about my house or April or you, for that matter.'

They'd had enough hugging for the day and when they'd finished their scones both women simply stopped leaning against Grace's car and each took to their own driver's seat. Grace's was black and Nic's red, both little hatchbacks and tough, although Grace could feel her engine start to give in or give over into something too full of friction and burnt things.

Nic tooted as she did a three-point turn and started on her way. Grace honked and then got out of her car, waving her arms and pointing.

'The tin!'

The red brake lights came on, and Nic retrieved the tin, giving Grace a wave.

The sea breaking on the rocks, the heather giving its stiff little shake in the wind, and this was them perched at the edge of summer. The risk of it. Grace felt it red and sore in her gums, in the churning of her stomach and, to her surprise, in the smile on her lips and the pure bright joy she felt rush through her for so many miles traveling south.

She saw a peregrine. Two deer up against the horizon. A reed bunting with his black head. She'd take the two job offers that were on the table. They were short stints, a few months only. Let April do what she would to her house. She had left it in stranger, less caring hands before.

As she traveled south, with this lightness within her, she looked at the land differently. Here you could farm. Here you could build a house. Here, she thinks, closer to her cottage, around a bend she doesn't usually travel, you could have a tiny bakery that would be just big enough.

Weeks of work and making excuses to Charlie, calling in favours from people she'd worked with over the years, mostly pulling Donald out of his sick leave/semi-retirement, and Nic had already laid the foundations of the house by the time she finally drove Charlie up to see the croft. They walked the rough road and he didn't understand. Even as they stood at the top of the land, with the foundations in front of them and the sea beyond.

'This is mine,' Nic said.

And he didn't get it. She ran forward and stomped a foot on the house's foundation.

'This. I own this. I made this.'

His face was something. Crumpled, wrecked. Something other than she'd seen there before. Charlie turned around and left. Walked right off through the muir towards the road. She let him go. Heat rushed to her cheeks and her chest. A fury. He had a thumb and he could use it.

She sat on her land and nothing had changed. Too often as kids they'd looked at their dad just waiting to hear where he would take them next. Where would they have to follow, like ducklings, like lambs? Where was that patch of land they could rely on? Where were the people they could rely on?

Charlie struggled, he said later that night as they sat in the living room of his flat, with something he didn't know he would struggle with. He thought it was his duty, as the man, to build the house, the home. 'Dad has failed me and Mum so badly, I'd sort of promised myself I'd do better.'

'You will.'

'You've not given me the chance.'

'I didn't think...'

She started to soften and somehow that was worse for Charlie, because he wasn't telling the whole truth. Something else was going on too.

'But I think mainly it's some old-fashioned sexist thing in me.'

'What do you mean? You need to be the man?'

'I can't have a woman own my home.'

Her sympathy lessened.

'That's ridiculous.'

'I know.'

'Best if we knock that one on its head,' she said.

That night there was no top or bottom but both and neither and that's how they'd go forward. And that night the condom broke.

'Fuck.' They both said it. 'Fuck.'

CHAPTER 12

The sun shone and heat built and Ben was a sweaty hot mess by the time he got off the bus. He couldn't remember his dreams but that woman's comment had shaken him. What he fancied was a long, demanding swim in a place where, if you swam too far out, the sea might take you. Such an effort it would be to pull yourself back. It was a game he used to play on days when death and life were all mashed up together in him. He'd risk it, today, swimming past the muscle burn and past the first wind and second and third winds until there was no more. He'd let his lungs give out and his body, and he'd be at sea.

He closed the taxi door and his feet took him without thinking towards the bar where April worked. He could handle an hour with her, and then he'd take a decisive action and never again have to see that look in his family's eyes. It was worse than hatred. Worse than being despised. Because he knew, even now, as he made plans he'd keep, it was harder to see their love for him hold hands with disappointment.

Some folk who didn't know Col were talking to colleagues who did when they thought Col was out of hearing range. Col often heard the chatter and reserved the right to pay no attention at all. On most days , Col wasn't made or unmade by other people's opinions.

Col moved further into the open, where there was a proper signal, and called April about seeing her today, perhaps for lunch at The Still, and she said yes.

'My brother might be here, and I'd love for you to meet him.'

After seeing them together at the pub at New Year, Col had mixed feelings about Ben, augmented by a wise, learned trepidation about brothers more generally. Col hadn't seen Innis for twelve years. This was an acceptable arrangement on both sides.

Those troubled teenage years. The angst. The uncertainty. All the change of your twenties. Who wanted to go back and re-hash all that?

'Any time that suits,' April said. 'And then we have all night.'

'Perfect.'

Col hung up and the chatter had turned to laughter. Col didn't turn around or assume their laughter was directed in this direction.

Here Col was almost where Col wanted to be. For almost fifteen years, it'd been a process of shifting, and it's one that hadn't quite settled, which annoyed Col who believed that, at thirty, some of these things should have been resolved already.

Col was born she. Then, for a while, Col was neither and both and had settled on they. For the past few years, Col had been passing as *he* and it was easier, in many ways, but that old churn of self-not-being-self had started again and Col had been shifting back to both since the spring. April had perhaps started to notice this movement but hadn't known what she was witnessing, not for sure.

'I couldn't quite put my finger on it,' she' had said last night. 'But I liked it.'

It was a start. They'd talked, a bit, into the early hours. It would be part of a longer conversation, hopefully over weeks, months, years. Words were a blunt instrument, still not up to the task; Col sought the best way to say what it was that was going on. April was there, having a conversation she'd never once imagined she'd be a part of, but she understood from her own experiences that you can know who you are and yet the world sees something else and feels free, very free, to call you what it likes and to beat you up. April said she enjoyed being herself, but facing the world could be exhausting. She mentioned that Col didn't seem exhausted.

Col walked back into the group and they got back to work and this practicality let the air settle on things they understood and agreed on. Another hour or so and they'd be done. Later, April would be in the bar, democratic with attentions to the customers, except perhaps for the extra warmth with which she'd welcome her brother, and maybe Col too.

April was propping open the door to the pub and putting the chalkboard menu sign out on the pavement when she spotted a tall, familiar man who looked beaten up.

'Oh here's Big Ben.' She looked at him and beckoned him into the pub leading them to the bar, where he half-sat on a bar stool. His bag dropped like a body beside him. 'What gorse thicket did you stumble into?'

'His name was Andy and he got much worse than he gave. This,' here Ben waved his hand around his face, 'is all from after they were holding back both my arms.'

She poked at him, at his shoulder and his ribs. He winced, but barely, being brave. It was enough, she was his sister and she knew.

'If you got him good, and you're in this state, is he in the hospital?'

'Thankfully, no. Or I'd not be here but in an Aberdonian jail.'

'Seriously?'

'That's me off the rigs.'

She put her arms around him. He was becoming barrel-bodied like their dad, but taller, a big guy and yet she could hold him and it would do something, she was sure of it. When she released him she kept a hold of his arm and hand, pressing her forearm along his.

'Did you tell Nic you'd knocked out a guy?'

'Not yet.'

'So what are you going to do now?'

'I'm hoping that one of my siblings might offer me their couch or spare room.'

'Nic will be here in a couple of hours. She's got room.'

'Ouch.'

'Don't ouch me. You're a big man, you'd have to fold

yourself twice over to fit on my couch.'

'You could give me your bed.'

'Fuck right off, mister. You start a punch-up…'

'Who said I started it?'

'Me knowing you, that's what tells me you started it.'

Ben shrugged and grinned.

'And you got yourself fired.' April paused, connecting the dots, tapping at his wrist. 'Ah. I get it.'

'I'm not saying I did it intentionally.'

'But you didn't swerve away from it.'

'Definitely not.'

Taking a step back, he straightened but pushed up his sleeve. April folded back the bandage. The marks were like prison markings—IIII and / cutting through them.

'I've been meaning to ask.'

'Why didn't you?'

'Because I'm a lazy sod. I've had my own mess, you know.'

'Yeah, who are you to talk? You've been fired more often than me, and with punches thrown too.' They laughed. 'We're a couple of bruisers. A recovery pint, sis?'

'Have you had breakfast?'

'I was rushing here to see my family.'

April moved behind the bar, raised the first order of the

day—a full cooked breakfast, double bacon, fried eggs, and white toast for her brother. And then she pointed to each tap in turn until he nodded and poured him a pint.

Back around the other side of the bar, she lifted his bag, ignoring his 'That's heavy!' and the implicit 'You're a girl', and carried his bag to the back room, to make way for the paying customers who would arrive any minute, en masse, as if a bell had been rung. Every day, people crowded into the pub carrying their shopping, dragging their bags and friends and family. Eyes scanned the same bottles hers had, looking for soft drinks or seeking out the espresso machine. Planning what would suit them best.

She was back and ready. Ben moved to the stool at the end and blended in and April watched the bar and the door, thinking about last night waiting for Col to arrive. The world, this world, you couldn't predict it.

After Grace received Sonny's text she immediately took to stomping the bracken into submission. Then she fixed the chicken wire along the bottom of the southern portion of fence, twisting the wires and closing the gaps. Digging up the tenacious ground elder, she was ruthless, leaving big gaps where she forked the soil to follow all the fleshy white roots. Sun beat down and she sweated and swore. She didn't want to make Viv feel unwelcome. But she wasn't welcome. After this long away, you ease your way back, you don't show up at a family reunion and expect people to be happy. In her head she tried out different wordings to respond to her sister. No swearing, she coached herself. Understand her point of view. It's probably taken her years to work up to this. Maybe she's better, maybe she's sought help. Maybe she's run out of money. Maybe she's been nurturing resentment and rage and she'll bring a match and torch the place. Grace's head pounded with the heat. Sweat rolled down her neck and along her spine. There was a woozy feeling and she knew she needed to rehydrate. Her gardening gloves flapped to the ground when she let them go and she wiped her filthy feet on a towel she'd left at the entrance. Clean enough. She stood at the kitchen counter drinking one glass of cold water and then another. The tone of the day had tilted and she was unsure of how to tilt it back. When she heard Sonny's car coming round the bend, she took out the toolbox from the cupboard. It was too early for beer on what would be a marathon day and so she put the kettle on and took two mugs out of the cabinet. There was work to do, strategies to put in place. There was family to prepare for.

Sonny stepped out of the car and onto the land and it was like a switch was pulled. Here he let down his guard and was himself. He'd always liked Grace but he didn't let it show too much - it'd go to her head. Her practicality was reliable. It was made real in how in her kitchen everything was planned. And the rest of the house, well, it was the rest of the house. She used to leave the toolbox for him to trip over on the first morning after they'd arrived and he'd find the things that needed to be fixed and he'd fix them. She always had cold beer in the fridge.

As he walked up her front path he could hear the kettle boiling and he couldn't really imagine the shape of the coming conversation. Viv was going to come home at some point and they'd need to be ready for her.

CHAPTER 13

Welcome, Finn

When Nic confirmed with Charlie what they had both believed to be true for weeks, Charlie gestured his thumb north towards her croft and those nice little foundations she had poured: 'Well that puts a timescale on the thing.'

All the plans, and then the body took over and the girl was pregnant.

Nic became a machine. She worked through the morning sickness, the constant dizziness and churning of her gut. In bed at night she called it a headache but it was stranger, and she often had to close her eyes, because of the pain, sure, but also because of how sometimes she had her own northern lights at the edges of her peripheral vision. Sometimes her vision tunnelled to a narrow strip but she thought that was her focusing all her energies on getting the house built before the baby came. And she was tired, sometimes lying down in the field, in the middle of the floor, pushing the seat of the car back for a snooze. Her friends who were mothers said it was normal, but it didn't feel normal. It felt foreign and extreme.

She sent out a gentle call for help in exchange for IOUs and good food and crack. Friends from Uist arrived, telling her how much she'd done for them in previous years. At the time it had always just felt like living. She'd reacted against the inaction she saw in her dad and had found her own ethics: never leave someone by the side of the road; never stand back if you can step forward; don't be a doormat; say yes to every opportunity you can—if not you'll miss this life, and it's a short one.

They focused their energies on the house and getting a roof over their heads. The rare times she'd spoken with her dad, despite him knowing their plans, where they were and their need for help, he'd expressed a dogged persistent opinion about her going into teaching or nursing, just as he had been vocally against her apprenticing with Donald or working on the ferry. Eventually he suggested she keep hens or maybe start a crèche to make the crofting commission happy. She'd grown tired of trying to explain it to him.

'Were you like this with mum?' She thought about all the housework, all the laundry, taking care of them and working outside the house too.

'What do you mean by that?'

'Nothing, Dad, nothing.' They could have used his

knowledge and help, but she didn't invite him up.

Ben, April and Grace made regular trips up. Initially, they drank more than was useful and she'd had to chastise them. After that they knuckled down and were more productive.

Together, and with generous gifts of wood and bits and pieces that people would bring as they came to help out, they made it compact and lovely: three small bedrooms and a wee open-plan living room, dining room, kitchen area downstairs. Wood-framed and packed with insulation. Turns out Charlie had been a saver too and it was a nice surprise.

'Sly dog.'

'It's not much.'

'It helps a lot.'

They spent a quarter of the budget on windows within a solar-capture design, but would have to save for solar panels. Playing the long game. They'd agreed she'd stop working at CalMac, because the shifts made real progress on the croft untenable. Nic wasn't yet sure how she'd make her living and she needed running costs to be as cheap as humanly possible.

She built some stone walls with the rocks they kept digging up and planted a tester garden within the square boundary, off to the side, to see how things grew here. Of course her pregnancy grew bigger, a pressure, a physical change, that's the way it always happened, and each physical task took longer, was blocked by the ballooning of her belly.

The physicality of pregnancy defined Nic in a way she'd never been defined before. It made her diminutive as she fulfilled what felt like a predestined role. It comforted people who looked at them, who had thought that maybe she was a dyke because of how she dressed and moved and acted and the work she did, and now she was tamed, less threatening, familiar. She had never known the concern she'd caused before as a single woman, the threat she'd posed. Grace would understand it. They'd never talked about it, and probably never would. But Nic knew it now. She thought she should feel free but instead the role felt small and restrictive. So she kept moving and working and doing everything as before until the very last minute when her body shouted to her that it was impossible. She moved past that. And again. Until Charlie took the tools from her hand with one hand, as the other rested on her belly.

'Nic, I won't tell you to stop. But slow. Take a pause. This baby needs you to be everything. Everything you are but safer.'

He said it and she took it seriously because he'd stop rock climbing, was going to sell his motorcycle; knew he was important here too. They needed all of him, but safer. His loss would be catastrophic, and if he brought it on himself that would be unpardonable.

Charlie was away for a fortnight at a time and Nic was alone. He'd take extra shifts too, when asked, because they'd agreed they needed the money. The baby in her belly kicking her like a conscience, *You thought this would be a good idea, why?*

Ben was flying out to the rigs, and incommunicado, and so she texted her sister: *This was supposed to make us happy.*

April was eating dinner with a small dram in a tasting glass just to the right of her plate. A Speyside, a mid-week smooth whisky that somehow Grace got cut-price from a friend who worked in IT for a few distillers or something.

Happy? My sister wants to be happy? April was suspicious of the word somehow and reached over for the dictionary Grace kept by the kitchen table for occasions just like this. The definitions of happy were decidedly reserved, could even be considered grumpy, and were all about appearances versus being.

Happy: 'well-adapted, appropriate, felicitous' and 'cheerful, willing' or 'enthusiastic about or involved with to a disproportionate degree.'

That's the best we can hope for? Some sort of appropriate but begrudging, overly saccharine, false cheerfulness?

It's bullshit.

She texted her sister:

Happy? Aim higher. This is what Collins has to say. And she sent her the definitions.

I'm buggered, Nic replied, *if happy isn't even good enough. Can I settle for miserable and foolish?*

On the way to happy in the dictionary I found this, maybe you should grow one, or have Charlie do it.

April sent Nic the photo she'd found: a close-up of a man with a handlebar moustache, a huge grin plastered on his face. It was ridiculous and brilliant.

Mum always wanted dad to grow a moustache and a beard.

But he refused, said they were 'A bunch of unhygienic nonsense'.

'But cute,' Mum would say.

Even when they weren't fighting they were cringe-worthy. What do you think about moustaches?

No opinion. I wish I could snap my fingers and the baby would be here and the other building would be built and I could get on with things.

April laughed so hard at this that she knocked over her glass.

You think that's how this works?

April texted Charlie the definitions and the photo too. *Your wife thought the croft would make you both happy. But I think this would do the trick.*

By the time he got home he was two weeks into quite an impressive moustache and Nic laughed so hard she peed herself a little.

Another summer deluge flooded the whole of the north and, in a sudden heat at dawn, the world turned to steam.

Charlie stood at the car as his wife approached with her hospital overnight case in one hand and their shared luggage slung over her shoulder. They were going to spend the days before her due date at Grace's, which was closer to the hospital. A visit precipitated by pre-birth nerves.

He had just fitted the babyseat they would need on the way back, and had offered to come back to the house for the bags. She refused his help, and on this absurdly tropical day she was glowing with the effort. Charlie wouldn't be surprised if this baby was born on the trot. He cautioned Nic but she was having none of it. She wore the lightest dress she had—an unfeasibly brightly flowered sundress: maternity-wear. He held up his phone to take a picture or maybe even a movie of the woman he loved bedecked in bright pink flowers.

'Do not. Charlie. Just don't.' She put down both bags. Her anger was an excuse, he was thinking. 'Take your finger off that trigger. If you must, take a picture in your head. Here, I'll give you a gift.' She stuck out her bump and placed a maternal and yet somehow pornographic hand on her belly. She flipped her hair and did a turn for him. 'Speak not a word of this Mr Skirving, not to a soul. Even this dress will be a secret between you, me and my close relatives.'

The car rattled down the rain-darkened roads and steam rose from the tarmac. They'd hit the road early to do everything Nic wanted before the baby arrived. Heavy puddles turned to mirages as they travelled south. The hottest day either could remember. Hotter than memory could hold. And it was barely even 8am.

With Nic's overnight case in the boot of the car, Charlie's driving had no urgency to it, not too much speed, and he didn't swear at stupid drivers, most of them tourists, who did 20 on the curves and then raced up to 70 on the straights, making it impossible to pass. Or the motorcyclists with death wishes. Nic let her legs fall wide and she held her arms away from her torso like she was sunburned or wearing a dress with pins in it. Air. Get all the air moving.

He said nothing, pulled in once or twice to admire the view, let Nic stretch her legs, get a breeze blowing through that skirt of hers. He liked the look of her in a dress but had more sense than to tell her. She'd already been furious at so much about this pregnancy. The raw animality of it. Don't tell her it was powerful and awe-inspiring. He'd learned that by watching a friend of theirs try and she was a mother of four kids.

Nic had replied, 'No, I'm the fucking massive beast who's going to be pushing a little beast out my fanny.'

Charlie and Nic used to pride themselves on being friends who took fussy babies and did their best with them, who didn't shy away from changing nappies and burping even the most enthusiastic throw-uppers. But certainly there was a point at which they simply handed the little buggers back, with a kind but firm shrug of the shoulders that said, *They're yours.*

Now they knew that they'd soon have their own uncontrollable person who they'd legally and morally have to take home no matter how she or he was behaving.

Nic was anything but tired when they got to Grace's, and she opened all the windows as soon as they arrived.

'Yeah, sure, don't mind the midges,' Grace said, the trees stock still except for the heat-humid slow-droop.

Then Nic looked around and found things to fix and meddle in. A tetchy cabinet that needed WD40; a door handle that wobbled; anything that didn't require Nic to get down onto her hands and knees. Even this superwoman had her limits.

Grace tugged at the frayed fabric of her favourite chair. Nic was trying to find space in the cramped house for all her worry, all her hope, and the cool air she wanted to magic up on a day that was set to fry them.

'You could make space shaving off Charlie's ridiculous facial hair. I've left the clippers and a razor on the sink,' Grace suggested.

'Not a fan of the moustache?' Charlie said to her holding both curled ends aloft.

'If you were aiming for hipster, you missed.'

'I'll have you know this is a handlebar moustache and it's a classic.'

'It's definitely one for the history books.'

'Nic likes it.'

'It's ridiculous and that makes me happy. And when he grins, this one in here does flips.'

Charlie grinned and Nic said, 'See?' She pulled the fabric of her dress taut and you could see ripples. 'Now where is that brother of mine. Him and his promises. I should know not to trust Ben to be on time. He'd want to see this.'

April arrived from some task she was calling a job and her arms stretched around her sister, briefly rubbed the wings of her shoulder blades.

'You look amazing.'

'What, little old me?' Nic shook her head but didn't challenge her.

Charlie stepped forward. April reached up and kissed Charlie on his hair-capped lips, grinned and turned to Nic: 'Adorable, I think his handlebar is adorable.'

'Me too,' Nic said. 'Now hands off.'

'No worries. I prefer my men clean-shaven.'

'That's how I like my women too,' Grace yelled from the kitchen.

'Just as well,' Charlie said pointedly to April. 'I prefer my women to have tact. And their own digs.'

'I have my own room. I pay rent.'

'I mean somewhere you can swing a cat.'

'Or get that tache in the door.'

'Or squeeze this in,' Nic gestured to her belly.

'Yeah,' April said, bending down and speaking to their bump. 'When you coming out to meet us, sprog?'

Ben was traveling up from London, where he'd been doing some hideous management training and there had been a bus replacement between Dunkeld and Pitlochry. Finally past that, the train was just going over the Drumochter pass, and he craned his head to see if the outline of any deer stood out along the top of the hills. He was six hours behind schedule, what with delays and everything, and his phone was dead and his charger was buried in the bottom of his bag, shoved behind at least a dozen other bags near the doors. Hours ago he'd wanted to call Nic to let her know how late he'd be. Why was he the one to get a train which only had OAPs and the families with small kids? Where were the unruly teenagers, the greasy-haired stoners, the people who never shut up, who would let him borrow their phone in exchange for a beer or the promise of a fag?

He had been struggling. He hated the job, the rigs, the gaping chasm of any worth whatsoever in what he was doing. Sonia's voice. She'd not been wrong, she simply had bad timing. He hadn't had enough savings to give Nic what he'd promised and so had taken out a loan, which he could get because he had a job, but wouldn't tell her or Sonia that. Sonia had left him because he stayed on the rigs, saying it showed his bull-headed selfishness. Why bother to try to set it right?

He thought he could talk through the Sonia thing with Nic and all the stuff it'd churned up. At first glance you'd think it would be April he should talk to, with her losing her job and all that, but she didn't understand struggle. She found herself within a maelstrom and thought, *bugger*, first, maybe for a second and then *how interesting. How fascinating. Look at how everything is whipping around me in a total mess.* She would be drinking and joking the next day like it was nothing. Sometimes he wondered if she had low blood pressure or a thyroid issue and whether she was truly unexcitable in the normal ways. He wondered if that swing had done some sort of permanent damage when it knocked her out cold. He never said, because Nic still took that accident way too seriously. She took loads of things way too seriously and she seemed to be worn down by how elusive a foothold up north was proving to be, especially with this year's bad weather.

They flew past the white buildings of the Dalwhinnie Distillery and his chest felt a historical sort of warmth, a thirst for a dram. But the train powered past. And Newtonmore, Kingussie. The increasing sprawl of Aviemore. The air grew thick and hot and he sat sweltering. When the doors opened, hot humid air compressed the compartment. The train gave incredible vistas of rocky dark mountains still with touches of snow in the north-facing corries, of tiny Victorian stations, and through the backsides of the smaller places where much of life is lived and it looked cluttered. He remembered being on an Amtrak crossing the Rockies and remote campers mooning the train with white globes for butt-cheeks. The guides tried to move everyone move to the windows on the other side of the train. *On this other side there's no moon but we can still see clearly*, one said.

It was just after 11pm when the train pulled into Inverness. He checked his wallet and got into a taxi. Grace's cottage was dark but for the porch light and a single light in the kitchen. He saw the note on the table through the door window. There was only one car in the driveway. His hand was on the handle and Ben was at the table in two long, swift steps.

A catch, a catch.

The note was in Nic's fantastically barely readable scrawl. *Where they hell have you been? We're up at the loch for a midnight swim. No suit needed! Unless you've gone shy.*

Ben sprinted. His legs had rarely felt happier and lighter and stronger. At the banks of the loch he stripped off his clothes. His family were barely visible patches of skin in the moonlight, all moving into the deeper, colder and fresher water.

'Hey. Hey. Hey,' he shouted as he ran, arms flung out to the side, ready to flap as he took to the water at speed.

'Whoop. Whoop. Whoop,' he heard in response.

Bugger if the cold of the water didn't half take all the wind from you. His ribs contracted. How was Nic in here at all? This was definitely nothing like a bath. The air though, was hot and wrapped you up. She moved towards him and he made his way through the water to meet her.

'We're not long here. I'm making for shore soon.'

'If this doesn't get labour going I'm not sure what will.'

Charlie swam-walked beside her. 'Hey Ben, good to see you. We were worried.'

But Ben could see that that worry was tiny and hidden beneath and behind about a hundred others he had.

April and Grace had gone far out into the water, in a dare or for pure pleasure or something.

'We've been calling and calling,' Nic was saying. Ben laughed. 'Okay, so we tried once and figured you'd get here when you get here.'

'And I got here.'

The water poured off her and Ben couldn't believe the roundness of of Nic's belly and he wondered how her skinny legs could hold her up. Charlie handed her a big robe he pulled from a beach bag and she pulled it tight around herself and laughed.

'I'll be a big ball of sweat in two minutes, but for now, it's perfect.'

Charlie took out another towel, dried himself and handed it to Ben. 'Sorry mate, we only have the two.'

'It'll do.'

They were all more shadow than light and Ben imagined

this bubble of love around the two of them: secure, bedding down for a new era.

Grace and April had reached some sort of destination, whatever that had been, turned in the water and you could hear their voices as well as their slow, messy strokes through the water heading for shore too.

Looking up, the sky seemed to fall through the trees, summer just-dim night settling like haar. Rest coming into his bones.

Charlie placed an arm around Nic, turning them both towards the path down. 'I'm getting her down the hill and into bed. No matter what she says.'

'I'll walk down with you. I'm famished and parched.'

'I'll go down but I'm not sleeping until this one and me have done some talking.' Nic hooked her arm through Ben's briefly, before disengaging to fan herself with her hands.

'And I've had some grub and a beer.'

'A glug for me too.'

Almost a tut from Charlie. Nic shot him a look like they'd talked about this. Watch it.

'We're heading back,' they shouted. Grace and April must have heard but gave no sign. Down the path they went, Nic accepting Charlie's hand. Halfway down, as the heat built again, she let loose the tie and her robe fell open. Charlie said nothing. Ben didn't look, only a glance, and saw the things that nature puts us through. There was nothing in his sister's pregnant body that looked comfortable. Nothing at all.

And yet, as they all sat and talked, clothed once more, Nic in a dress, of all things—she said nothing of her body, of these months, just the frustration of the delays of the build, the house up, but the internal fittings not yet complete. They had sinks and a toilet and a stove. Electricity was in but not all the sockets were connected.

'You think we're here for the hospital. But we're not. We're here for the soft bed and the home-cooked meals.'

'And the craic.'

'Bring it on.'

Nic and Charlie drank water and snacked on toast and Marmite and then went to bed, Nic tugging on Charlie's arm, gentle shadows having formed beneath her eyes. Ben sat drinking beer and looking out over the fields and, when Grace and April arrived, out came the vodka and they stayed up until the small hours, drinking beer after beer with neat shots bolstering their talk of sports and books and politics, setting the world to rights, agreeing, disagreeing, and avoiding any familial topics. They went to bed and the next morning there was a quiet in which a shared headache boomed right beside Nic's white-knuckled anticipation of a life about to change.

In the end Nic's waters broke on Grace's living room floor, and the birth was long and messy but pretty straightforward as these things go.

Ben had been called away to work the day Nic went into labour, to a place he couldn't divulge, and left without getting to meet Finn. A promotion he had taken meant more travel, more dangerous work. Nic didn't understand the choices he was making.

'Your job just gets dodgier and dodgier,' Nic said a few days later, holding Finn up to the phone.

'Tell me about it.' Ben said. 'Another story for a different phone call. Oh, he's cute.'

'Thanks, darling.'

'By which I mean he looks nothing like you.'

'Hey you, be nice. He's bigger than a football.'

'You both look beautiful and I'm sorry not to be there.' He scanned his phone around his motley crew of co-workers who were hanging out in a bar by the looks of it, and a few of them made rude gestures.

'Nice,' she said. 'Charming.' Was it just her or did she see more of their father in him? His eyes dulled, his wit simplified.

Whispering. 'I mean it, sis, he's gorgeous. I really wish I could have stayed longer. We'll get on, Finn and me, I can tell.'

'It's his little fists, isn't it?'

'How'd you guess?'

Her dad arrived and worked in the garden and drank beer. Nic was barely in the door with Finn when her dad raised the question about whether they should tell Viv about her first grandchild.

'No,' Nic and April said in unison, sharply.

'Remind me never to cross the two of you,' Grace laughed.

Sonny shook his head dismissively.

'Why,' Nic said, 'when she's missed so many other things, would I include her in this?'

'Because she's your mother. Because this could be an opportunity.'

'What? For reconciliation?'

'She could be some help. She had three kids.'

Nic and April groaned. Not bothering to argue about this again.

'It doesn't work like that, Sonny,' Grace said.

'Why? Why wouldn't it?'

'Because she's Viv.'

With her newborn wrapped tight against her, Nic went to the counter and drank some juice from the fridge. Finn grew tetchy and she and Charlie tried to soothe him. The rest of her family made noises and moved around them but it only made her feel watched. There was no one in the room who had ever taken care of a newborn before. At night Nic read how-to books and scrolled through websites. It would have to be enough.

The next day Charlie took the bus to Ullapool to start his two-week shift and Sonny attempted to broker a peace but eventually left a day earlier than planned. Nic stayed at Grace's so April and Grace could help her out with Finn for just a bit longer. She stayed one extra day and then another. Eventually, Grace was due for a stint on a yacht in France, and April had been going to work the whole time. Finally, Nic had to face the croft, motherhood, everyone, everything, alone.

As she packed the car, with Grace holding Finn, her body shook gently, a nervous heckling that came from her very core. She was determined to be nothing less than she was before. And to do everything she had done before.

Don't think too much about it, just do it, Grace whispered.

'I could pack my bags and come with you,' April said, half-turning back to the house to do it, but Nic took Finn from

Grace and put him in his car seat. Crying and not looking back at her sister and aunt because she'd say yes if she looked. She'd say yes and she had to do this alone.

Three hours later Nic texted from Ullapool. *You'd be yelling at me April, for driving so slow. It's nerve-wracking having him in the car. What a responsibility. And plus I kept having to pee, so badly, too often. And feed him. Fuck. Fuck. Packing up again now, another hour.*

Two hours later. Another message. *Home safely. All good. He likes the cot, which is a relief. Charlie left a love-heart note taped to the front door handle. We'll be fine. We're fine. Love to you both.*

Later, April would think this is the last time her sister ever expressed any doubt or concern. She must have still felt it, but she stopped sharing it.

CHAPTER 14

April looked across the counter of the bar at her cheeky brother, and texted Nic. *Ben's here and he's all beat up.*

What?

'Smile, dude.' And Ben grinned, pointing to the worst cut, and April snapped a photo. Sent it.

'You have a signal?' Ben asked.

'Of course.'

His phone was still without bars. 'I need to change carriers.'

That looks painful. Nic texted. *Did he start it?*

What do you think?

'Tell her to get her arse down here.'

'She's just sent a picture of her and Star in the garden. Says she's thinking of taking a nap.'

'Tell her to clean the dirt from under her nails and come see her family.'

'Done.' April poured a few pints, delivered a food order to the table, came back. 'Finn's nursery took an outing today and they'll meet at the Achiltibuie pier at 4:30. They decided to let him go because he was so excited. So it'll be six or so before they're down.'

'I suppose she wasn't expecting me and so there'd have been no reason to rush.'

'How did that ego of yours fit through the door? I'm surprised the weight of it doesn't break the stool.'

She texted Nic a teaser: *I hooked up with someone last night.*

Not the creepy one?

No, a beautiful one.

Will I get to meet him? Give my approval?

Don't need your approval. But, maybe, yes. Might have to work, travel. We'll see.

You're a tease.

Go pick up Finn and get yourselves down here. The loch is waiting.

Two Highland Park poured for an older couple who had a Leakey's Bookstore canvas bag and a bag of food, a carton of eggs precarious on the top.

'A bit early for a dram isn't it?' Ben said once they'd taken their glasses and sat down at a table a wee ways away.

'It's never too early for a dram,' added Aly, April's boss, arriving and immediately joining the fray.

'That's greed speaking.'

'Don't get him started. I'm intervening. Aly, Edith over there needs a refill, and you could gather her plates, sweet talk her a bit. Her old man is in the hospital and she's always had a bit of a shine for you.'

Aly was just placing a glass of the house white on Edith's table as Col walked in.

April's laughter travelled through the room, like a warbler's call, from the end of the bar where she was with her brother. Col continued towards the bar, but the other end, not wanting to pressure her. They hadn't talked about any of that. It was just one date, one night.

Aly came up beside and put a hand to Col's shoulder, 'What can I get you?'

'A bottle of IPA, please.'

'I'll get it,' April said and came to the end of the bar, placing one hand on the nap of Col's neck, pressing their bodies together.

'But first, come meet my brother, Ben.'

She led the way. Ben stood to greet them, his face a testament to some recent battle, survived.

They shook hands and Ben half-flinched at the grip, his knuckles bruised too.

'You should see the other guy,' Ben said.

'I can see you. Are you the winning side, or otherwise?'

'Who is this guy to be asking that?' Ben asked April.

Sonny arrived and joined the fold. He put a hand on Ben's shoulder, who flinched slightly at the intimacy from his dad, and then Sonny shook Col's hand, infuriatingly winking at April.

Did either of them look at Col's fingers or wrists or hips or anything else for that matter?

'Nice to *finally* meet you,' her dad said, playing the concerned, interested father.

She could kick him. Absolutely kick him. He'd only guessed at Col's existence this morning and had never bothered about whom she'd dated before, except to pass negative judgements. She'd wait for it here too.

'Are you joining us for dinner?'

So, her dad was playing the long game.

Col smiled a warm, non-committal smile. 'That's a question for April.'

That was the only answer that would be the right answer. 'Will you all be nice?' she asked, of her brother and father.

'What else would we be?'

'A bunch of embarrassing people who ask awkward questions of a near-stranger.'

'Who, us?'

'Yes, you.' She shrugged. 'We'll let you know about that very generous invite later on, when we show up or not.'

Ben winked at her and her dad seeing this, nudged him, nodded in approval. So they barely talked to each other but they would band together to harass her.

Col stood watching it all. April checked to see if there was any movement in Col's feet towards the door. There wasn't. Col also didn't grab at her possessively or make this conversation about them or last night or anything. It was clearly about the Avens family, all they said and didn't say, and Col was fine with that.

Ben went to fetch his bag, raising an eyebrow at April. What was in that question? What did he suspect? Know? See?

Her dad looked out of place, suddenly, amidst his kids and April's lover and he coughed. April put a hand on his arm, perhaps to give him a grounding.

'He seems nice,' Sonny said, leaning in.

She nodded, and April wondered if her dad would still be as neutral about her and Col later when it fell into place for him. But that wasn't for today. Not for here.

Col took the barstool Ben vacated, and sat through April's shift. Watching, talking, occasionally lending a hand, when she asked. They didn't know what they were yet. But each moment she felt Col beside her, she felt less need to ask that question.

Today she paid attention to comments made under breaths that she'd not listened for before. Side glances and stares as some customers tried to figure out what it was about Col that was different. They saw something that made them uncomfortable, perhaps. She often got similar whispers and, over the years, she'd tuned them out because they didn't define her. She only paid attention when the pitch of them rose or grew more insistent and the intention became risky and she needed to respond.

She too saw something unnameable in Col, and it was thrilling. She also knew she could be here as Col became something else, something even less definable, because she would be there too, altering, changing, in love.

CHAPTER 15

Hogmanay

April wound her way north. Her pathetic little car hated the ice and the snow and she was white-knuckling it from the first hill she hit outside Grace's. She couldn't decide which was worse: failing to get traction on the way up or failing to get traction on the way down.

The gloom, the gloom, the gloaming. The white of her hands in the heating that spat out fumes and a pathetic little offering of lukewarm air. She had on her three layers beneath her coat, plus a hat and scarf and fingerless gloves, with her fingertips almost numb to the touch. She turned down a side road, which was snow covered and compacted and so felt less potholed and then, out of the gloom, a tiny white house appeared, spilling warm light into the winter evening. April turned off her lights and coasted down into the spot beside the car parked there. Nic was inside lifting Finn out of his high chair, his face orange with neeps or sweet potato and his shiny hands clapped onto her sister's face, and she grinned. Kissing her son's lips and placing him down on his barely steady feet, she took the damp washcloth and wiped him clean as if he were a chalkboard. Halfway through he took the cloth from her and finished the job. He tugged on her shirt and she lowered him down and he pawed at her face with it too.

This scene of happiness wasn't everything. There'd been silence from Nic since Finn was born; even when they were together, she didn't talk about how she was finding motherhood. She'd talk about the house and workshop, sure, but not this wee'un, not the managing of a house and croft. April thought Nic's grin could be a mask for her son because that was what you do for kids. When she knocked on the door, Nic was surprised.

'We're expecting Ben. Did you pass him on the road?'

April thought back to the couple she'd passed, wrapped up against the weather. She couldn't say if one of them had been Ben. 'I don't think so.'

'How could you not be sure?'

'I wasn't looking for him.'

'We weren't expecting you yet but still recognised you when we saw you.'

'Do you want me to go get him, in the car?'

They both looked at the tiny car, that had barely made it here in the first place. The snow coming down.

'No, we'll all go on foot. From the bus stop he'll be cutting over the brae.'

'So he may not have been on the road at all.'

'Who am I to say?'

April put her lips together. What was it that her sister ever did say these days? She had alluded to both her and Finn having the flu.

'Are you both feeling better?'

'Yes,' said Nic quickly, dismissing her concern. 'Thanks for asking.'

There was only a half-hearted fence and, although the foundations for the workshop had been laid since the beginning, there was still no building. Her sister exhaled and looked at the useless foundations, where snow was falling, then she looked to the sky, out across the winter machair sweeping down to sea. April heard Nic's exhaustion and followed her sister's eyes down and then up. The snow swirled now, puffing like a smoker's exhalations in still, small gusts of wind. Growing heavy.

April's jaw ached, maybe with the weather. Her sister's curls were swept up into a wispy ponytail like their mum had worn and she actually had a skirt on, with leggings beneath, and wellies and high socks that looked so big they might even be Charlie's— the first ones she'd grabbed off the pile. Nic would have on a thin wool shirt, and at least two sweaters too, then her coat, which was almost a shawl and much too light for this weather. Although she felt the cold acutely, she got on with whatever she had to do regardless.

'Oh,' said Nic, calling Finn to her. As he approached, Nic started to turn in the snow with her hands and lips opening to the sky as she skirled and a mimicking son beside her spun with his arms wide and his mouth open to catch the snow. They gathered momentum, almost becoming dervishes and laughing. April watched, wanting her feet to shift and lift and turn and to be someone who saw snow and instantly was free within it. She found herself thinking, *I'm just not like that.* Her set jaw and crossed arms. It was a shock. Already at twenty-four she carried with her a belief that she was fixed, set in her ways and stuck with it all. She shook her hands and arms and let herself move in the snow, just to try it out. It felt false and forced at first and then, as warmth moved up through her body, she was free within it.

Nic stopped, her cheeks flushed, her breathing resolved. 'Let's go find uncle Ben.'

She checked her watch.

'Charlie's already docked,' she said, 'he should get home before the next front hits. Or, at least in time before it gets so bad we can't move.'

They walked to a good spot where they could see a figure with a head torch making its way towards them. They took a gamble and turned off their head torches. A game of hide and seek for Finn, and for Ben. 'You get to jump out and surprise Ben.' They waited, half-crouched, with her hand over his head torch.

The heather was high and so April would need to lift him up. The torchlight gave Ben's face shadows as well as brightness. She whispered, 'Now,' and Finn said 'Boo!' as April sailed Finn gracefully forward into Ben's path. He giggled wildly, the dark around them all-encompassing. On went each head torch until there were four weak beams. Ben took Finn, rubbing noses, kissing his cheek. The storm blew out its breath of snow and more snow. The house disappeared, the sea too. All directions swirled. Nic halted, turned, April behind her did as well, almost running into her sister. This was not familiar, they weren't sure how to be, and tension buzzed between the siblings.

Finn saw only snow. His laughter caught between the flakes. Snow everywhere and he wiggled to get down. Ben let him, thinking he'd head for Nic, but he didn't. He tottered free, wrapped up thick and puffy, and he stamped his feet, throwing up snow. How he ran. How he fell. Got up. Put up his arms. The wind gusted. The snow was icy and now the house reappeared, offering only a diffuse, distant light. Finn waved his arms like a bird and then he started to dance, his arms open, face turned up, cheeks red hot and gleaming with melting snow.

Ben sat on the couch with his socked feet on the table. Unhygienic, but they all did it. Finn was pressed into him, as if there was nowhere else in the world he'd like to be.

'I've got everything we need for a snow-in,' Charlie said crossing the threshold, holding the bags aloft before setting them down to receive his son who had clambered down and raced towards him. He breathed in the smell of him, the house, the Avens clan and took it all in his stride.

'Hiya, wee fisher.' Finn pressed his hot nose to his dad's cold cheek. Ben stood and the men hugged, friendly, stiffly. Charlie moved to April who had come to standing and he hugged her too. Charlie was bulky in the clothes he wore at sea, a thick, ambiguously coloured wool sweater frayed at the wrists, thick trousers, and industrial gloves laid across the bag he'd brought in. The hi-vis jacket would be in the boot of the car. He was generous to Nic's family, a spill over of the love he had for Nic.

'Good thing I picked up some treats,' he said. 'Just in case. And of course an extra bottle or two.'

'And?' Nic asked.

'Chocolate and crisps. Enough to feed an army of Avenses.'

'Okay then, I'll keep you,' said Nic.

Downstairs, Nic, Ben and Charlie were laughing as April tucked Finn into his new big-boy bed.

His eyes were open, clear and not quite ready for sleep.

April told him a story about a girl who loved to swim, which is a story she'd told before. Each time she told it, she'd weave in facts of their day. Sometimes she said, 'Bedtime voice,' keeping her voice soft and calm, running a hand through his hair, surreptitiously brushing his ear, as she'd heard it soothed babies, encouraged sleep.

She started the sleeping story, which was about a boy who liked to sleep, and she described each movement he made to get himself cozy in bed, the way the room looked with the light off. April turned off the light so they could better hear the sounds he could hear. Tonight they heard soft voices and laughter, with a substrata sound of pots and pans being negotiated in the kitchen. Family. Soon Finn was asleep and April lingered, listening to the sounds of the house and to Finn breathing.

Downstairs, Charlie had her coat laid out for her with a hat and gloves beside it. Grace was behind him, pouring both herself and April a dram.

'When did you get here?'

'Sonny showed up at my door and we decided to head up here.'

'In a blizzard?'

'We didn't realise that until we were halfway here.' Her aunt's eyes held a plea of sorts, *Please understand. I couldn't spend New Year's Eve alone with your father.* 'They're all out by the fire.'

'A fire in this?'

But the fire was hot before them and the night freezing at their backs. Conversation escalated about land ownership and what nationalism was—the things they argued about when they got together and some that had already been voted on—splitting the room each time. It was okay to a point and then drink and political righteousness threatened to take over. Viv had been the best arguer of them all, and there was something of her spirit here, but when Sonny mentioned her—when would he learn—it was clear that despite the fourteen years since she'd left it was all as raw as ever. They squabbled about every scrap of memory that had their mum in it.

'She only ever brought us trouble. And she brought out the worst in you too,' Ben said to his dad. He shook his head. 'She left us. Why can't you remember that? Why try to bring her back when it's clear she doesn't want to be here. She left us.'

Ben got up and went inside.

'Dad, you need to watch what you say around us,' Nic said. 'Sometimes we still want things from her she can never give. Like a conversation where she owns her mess. Or apologises. Ben needs that. Maybe April and I do too. She's a sore point. The Viv-shaped space is never not going to be tender or forgiven for us.'

They fed the fire and sat in silence.

'Dinner's ready,' Charlie called from the door. Calling them all around the same table, he must have thought himself a fool.

But, somehow, without discussing it, they gathered around the table for dinner and told stories about swimming and swings. Grace spun tales of obscenely rich and privileged singers with strange culinary and sexual preferences. She gave details. She was specific. Sometimes she gestured. Bellies ached, tears ran; Sonny squirmed but laughed too. Charlie talked about boats and the sea, and he could spin a good tale too. He didn't talk about his own family, which everyone knew was a sore point; when Nic asked him to, he sang a Gaelic fishing song. It was sturdy and beautiful and he had a fine voice for around a table.

His singing got them all started.

In questionable voices, there was more singing.

Nic was glad when she saw Finn's tiny figure, at the top of

the stairs, the safe side of the child gate, standing so very quietly, watching them sing and tell stories and bring in the new year.

CHAPTER 16

Chanterelles

It was the perfect day for mushroom picking—rain overnight and the chanterelles would emerge, and Finn, at three, was just old enough to have an obsessive eye. Nic got them going early, porridge in their bellies, a sneaky ginger cake baked early and now stashed in a tin with wax paper. She put apples, crisps, water bottles and her Swiss army knife into a thin cotton bag. They drove, taking their time heading down. In Ullapool they stopped for a hot chocolate and a wander and watched the ferry come in.

'Dad!' Finn shouted and Nic said, 'Yes, Dad's on a ferry, but not that ferry today.'

From a local weaver Nic bought Finn a thin wool sweater. 'This wool,' she told her son, 'comes from Eilidh's sheep. The ones in the field.'

'With the dog.'

'Yes, those.'

He chose a bright blue sweater with a sunflower on the front.

'My little sunshine,' she said.

She was pregnant again, she knew it. Only a few weeks, but she could tell because of the way her body was making space and being taken up simultaneously. Finn had all of her for three years, but soon he would have to share her with a sibling. She and Charlie had been slow with the progress of building the workshop and that would have to pick up. The only work she could find was in the local shop, such as it was, and there wasn't much else she could do, not with the wee one needing what she had, and the croft requiring her attention, and yet Charlie was starting to get anxious about how little money was coming in. And now this news. He'd been quiet, said he was pleased, but more worry, she was sure.

They'd had an informal warning from the Crofting Commission. It was a friendly nudge because they wanted young families, and those with the talents Charlie and Nic showed, but they still hadn't firmed up their plans for the business they hoped to run. They'd bought hens and let a neighbour graze her sheep on their land to pacify the commission; Nic circled and circled again around what she might want the outbuilding to become. Meanwhile she focused on the small family garden and the big task of raising Finn. Soon she'd have to focus on bringing the next baby safely into the world, but not yet. She and Charlie were fighting, a lot.

Why in the world did she think she could have the kids first?'

She could feel it all waiting for her: this perfect business, the money she'd make, the domestic happiness, and yet her body, this child before her, her playful, perfect little nymph with his shiny cheeks and mischievous eyes was what got all of her. She pulled him into a bear hug and kissed him all over. He raised his face for more kisses and she let him go before he felt even a hint of being held too long. And the next baby, not planned or avoided, would change things. Babies changed things. How foolish she was to have listened to her brother when he said she could do anything she wanted, in any order. The order mattered because once the kids arrived, nothing was the same.

They ate lunch by the tiny loch, sitting on rocks and not feeding the ducks. Finn threw a piece of cake that landed on the coarse small patch of sand. She made him run and pick it up.

'They can't become dependent on us,' she said. 'They need to find their own food.'

Small ducks on the water were already coming over, but Nic looked above and beyond them to a break in the woods where she could see the start of the hills to the southeast. Just the foothills, but even there the rock looked formidable. Before the ducks hit shore, she gathered all their things together and buckled Finn into the car for the short drive to the spot she was thinking of. Slowly winding their way along the single-track road, they passed people with binoculars hanging around their necks who walked its edge. She parked in a passing place. She'd heard from a friend that the chanterelles were good here. She helped Finn climb the low wooden stile. His trousers were tucked into his socks, hers too, but they had bare arms and held hands as they walked a barely there path a short ways into the old forest. The Scots pines were her favourites, with their red tinge and how each tree needed space and this made the canopy less dense and the woods more inviting.

The light today was magical, almost shimmering at the edges, as they made their way further into the woods. Finn dance-walked beside her.

'The mushrooms we're looking for will be here somewhere,' she said.

Finn pointed at a rock that, to be fair, did have a bit of a mushroom shape. 'Like this?'

'Close, wee fisher, but not quite.' She again showed him the laminated sheet for kids that had the photographs of mushrooms on it. 'This is what we're looking for. The ones you can eat on one side, the poisonous ones on the other.'

He looked at the picture and then at her. His dark head of hair and those endless brown eyes. He grinned.

'Okay.'

'And just these ones,' she said and pointed to the chanterelles. They walked side by side looking down. They picked a few and he seemed to understand that he was only to pick these mushrooms and they were to be cooked, so no nibbling. A lot of others couldn't be eaten at all. She said it and said it again.

She said some of their names.

Finn wandered a bit further away, searching. It's good to give kids space but she struggled, would continue to struggle, to let him out of her sight, to let him test his boundaries and sometimes fail. But as she watched Finn, the world slowed and darkened. She looked down, up, down. There were no mushrooms or wild flowers or tree roots on the ground, just patches of dirt and she couldn't understand it. The world had holes in it. She told Finn to be careful.

'Of what?'

'The ground,' she said. She heard him jump up and down.

'But it's just here mum.' She couldn't see him. She reached out to the nearest tree, and then squatted with her back against it. Rubbed her eyes. Something wasn't right with the light. She looked up and the woods looked dark, maybe a storm coming.

She felt a sense of dread too with the sudden dark.

'Finn, honey. Come to mum. Come a bit closer.'

Within seconds he was in her arms. She felt his hot cheek against her own. His wet kiss. His breath. She rubbed his back and mussed his hair.

'I found some,' he said.

And he opened her hands and put them in. She kept her left hand cupped and took her right hand and felt the outline of the tops and could feel their smoothness and the size was right but she couldn't bring it into focus at all. The strangest thing. The breeze was light and the day hot. Finn was standing between her legs as she squatted and he played with her ear, bumped his bum against her leg. What is real in this world? This child here. She didn't want to let him go.

'Mum is tired, Finn. Why don't we rest a little? Why don't we put away what we have?'

She shoogled out of her small rucksack.

'Have a look honey, there's a small paper bag in there.'

She heard him bend down: a crinkling of the bag. She opened her hand and he picked the mushrooms out of her palm one by one and dropped them into the bag. They hit it with a rustle.

'Okay sweetie, let's go back to the car.' Finn started to run ahead.

'Finn!' she shouted and tried to keep the fear out of her voice. 'Come here, come to Mama. I have a game I want to play.'

He raced up beside her. Put his hand in hers.

'Let's pretend mama is blind. And you're the smart boy you are. Lead me to the path and down to the gate.'

'Like I'm the boss.'

'Yes, like you're the boss.'

Nic thought he might be grinning and nodding too and she reached out and found his head, ran her hand over his hair.

'Make sure to tell me if there are stones or roots in my way so I can step over. Can you do that?'

'Yes. Yes.'

Finn took his job very seriously. He got them to the path, with its more compacted ground. He kicked rocks out of the way. Together they stepped over a few small branches that had been blown down by one of their many storms. He was a good guide and slowly the world opened again and there was her little boy holding his bag of chanterelles. They climbed the stile, and the world started to gain clarity and light with each step, and Nic once again became the mother guiding her toddler to the car. They were parked in a patch of sunlight and it was like a sauna in the car.

'How about a wee nap?' she said, seeing him rub his eyes

with his hands and his ear with his shoulder.

'No, mum, I want to see Grace.'

'Okay,' Nic said, but the day had worn them both out and when they got to the car she got into the passenger's seat, pushed it all the way back and stretched out. She cracked open all the windows and brought Finn into a hug and he curled into her, resting his head on her neck, his legs bent across and resting on her thighs. They rested there and then, inevitably, they slept.

Nic and Finn were due to arrive late afternoon and Grace left the bakery in capable hands to come and join them at her house. April was in the tiny back office at the bakery, attempting to help do the books. Grace chuckled. That girl was blustering her way through this life and it was painful to watch. She'd had the urge to slap April, hard, a real slap.

Nic parked the car carefully with the boot facing towards the house and turned to Grace as she got out to the car and waved. The young mother looked tired, her face a bit drawn, dark circles under her eyes. But the smile was true.

She went to the back seat and unhooked her son. He had a Thomas the Tank Engine engine, a paper bag that held something, a teddy bear and a book all clutched in his hands. It was amazing he could navigate anything but he found his way into Grace's arms. He was jaggy and soft.

Unceremoniously he dropped everything but the brown paper bag.

'I picked these,' he said, reaching down and taking up a few of the yellow mushrooms from the bag. 'Mum was sitting down to rest.' Finn put one hand over his right eye at this point and blinked. 'She said to only pick the yellow ones that had this,' and he showed Grace the flute of the chanterelles underneath.

'We'll double-check them,' Nic said as she leaned down and kissed the top of his head and then leaned over to give Grace a hug and a kiss.

He started to pull Grace around the house and wanted to go out into the garden. She looked to Nic.

'We played a game. He led me around the forest.'

Finn bent down and placed Grace's foot.

'He showed me where to step.'

'Ah,' Grace said. 'What a strange game. Here, let me help. You look beat up,' Grace said to Nic.

'That's how I feel. Would you mind looking after him for a while so I can take a nap?'

'Things okay?'

'Yes,' she said. Placing her right hand on her belly and then bringing a finger up to her lips. 'I think,' she said, 'early days.'

Grace reached out and touched her cheek. 'No wonder you look like you do.'

Grace pulled down the blinds in the spare room and pulled the curtains closed too. She smoothed the already smooth pillows and turned down the bed. Nic was standing outside, keeping an eye on her son downstairs. The two women traded places.

'Sleep well.'

'Thanks, Grace.'

Nic closed the door behind her and Grace walked down the twelve stairs.

'Okay, Mr Finn, you and me are going for a walk. You ready?'

He nodded.

She opened the front door and ushered him out. He jumped down her stairs, taking off and landing on two feet. Springing into the air, landing one step down. He didn't seem to want to hold hands and she went with that.

They saw a frog and she caught it, a tiny one, and he held it too. Gently. They heard a woodpecker and some trees creaking as the afternoon wind picked up a little bit. They could hear a chainsaw coming from one of the forestry tracks. They were felling some of the first woods they planted out here and she wondered when they'd get to this bit. She'd hoped not too soon. The clear-felled sections always looked like a disaster had struck.

'Ooh, the saws,' she said. 'The men have these machines that help them fell the trees. They're incredible, they do everything. This one machine can walk like this.' She used her hands as legs and made an awkward way over the ground. Finn imitated her and they laughed. 'These machines get to the tree they want, grip it like this,' and she opened her arms and grasped the air. 'They chop down the tree, slide the it through their arms to take off the branches, and cut the trunks into logs.'

Later that night April showed him a video of the real machines in action.

'Again,' Finn said, 'show me again.' And when he got tired of the video, he jumped up, keeping himself awake because everyone was here and he didn't want to miss this.

'I've got something to show you,' he said to April.

'And what is it?'

'Come with me,' and he pulled her up off her chair. She put down her glass and let herself be led.

He climbed up onto a stool, by the counter, that Grace had placed there, just for him. He pointed to the mushrooms they'd cleaned and were now spread out on paper towels. 'Mushrooms! Mama got tired and sat down, but I picked and picked and picked. She let me lead the way. Grace let me chop down loads of trees.'

Grace slept in the bedroom to the left of the top of the stairs, with Nic and Finn to the right and April down on the couch. Once the light was out, Nic opened the window and the curtain billowed in. Grace must have had hers open too and there was a lovely cross-breeze. The heaviness of the day had lifted, just a bit, although she'd been groggy all through dinner, her head slow and her movements too.

April had been on good form. She talked about jobs she'd been doing, focusing on the small catastrophes, weaving a tall tale of sorts. She and Grace were like a tag team. They complained about each other but there was love there.

Nic lay and thought about her sister and she didn't feel any worry about her for the first time in years. She couldn't say why. Finn turned into her, his head hot with sleep, his body too, and Nic freed them of the top blanket. Her own breath deepened and she thought about holding the cool metal swing in her hands and letting it go. It was an experiment. That arc ... could she catch it again? At first she hadn't seen April standing in the way but when she did, she hadn't shouted. Why didn't she shout? The small sound of metal and skull and then body and ground. April tells that story like it was a physics project, like she hadn't seen her, how the grin on Nic's face was all about the swing. If it'd been the other way around this memory would be a hard dark irritant for Nic, she knew it. Even a small sliver of doubt about her sister's intention would have twisted it all.

But April, she complained and hated just like the rest of them, resented and held grudges, and yet somehow time eased all that and a sort of alchemy of memory occurred. Not lies. Many of the details were the same—it was sunny and cool and the playground was in shade, they both remembered that. Nic had grinned, the sort of smile that comes over you and you might not even know why. April saw it and then was felled. And then she remembered passion in her sister's eyes, not malice. Nic wanted that sort of resilience for her kids.

When they woke up just after midnight there was a dark spot near Finn's eye. It moved. Little legs. Bugger, Nic thought. He was upset, almost hysterical.

'It's okay Finn, it's just a tick. It's okay, wee fisher. Come on. Try to stay quiet so we don't wake Grace.'

She wanted to carry him and take all the burden from him, but she didn't.

'Come on, honey.' She helped him off the bed and held his hand on the stairs and his breath caught, and again. She held his hand and he navigated each step, gulping in air, but more slowly. He calmed a wee bit and he tried, he was really trying.

April heard them and met them at the bottom of the

stairs, making faces at Finn.

'He has a tick,' Nic said.

'Poor thing,' and April went into the bathroom and found tweezers. Finn was small and clinging beside Nic and doing a great job of not touching his eye. He kept both eyes squeezed tightly shut. The tweezers were precise ones, sharp with a thin end. They'd do.

'Come on sweetie, come sit on my lap.' April invited Finn over and he went and she lifted him up and laid him down so his head was in her lap. She quietly placed her right arm over his body in a sort of hug that would also keep him still. Nic angled the light towards them both and kneeled in front of the couch and her son.

'Now honey, I need your help with this. You need to stay really still so I can be precise. It would help if you could hug yourself and try not to move.'

April ran a hand through his hair and started to whisper to him the story of the cutting machines, without the hand gestures. And what sound does the foresting machine make, she asked, and Finn whispered, keeping still, 'brrrrrr'd.'

Nic held the tweezers, such sharp objects, and took a good look at the burrowing wee beast. April pulled down gently on the skin beneath his eye to expose the tick. Right in the centre of the bottom lid where the lashes grow. Nic knew this was what you did for your kids, for the people you love. She knew how to do this. Right. She went in and made sure she grasped it low, so close to that liquid orb, her son's sight. She couldn't think about that. She grasped it close to the skin and gently and firmly pulled and twisted it counterclockwise and it came out first time.

'That's it, Finn. Brave boy.'

He blinked and sat up but stayed right in close to April. Then he leaned forward.

'Can I see it?'

Nic wanted to squeeze the little sucker between her fingers. Instead she held out the tweezers and the thing moved. She put it on a book and crushed it with the side of the tweezers. 'You need to kill them or else they come in for a second go.'

Finn pressed his thumb into April's arm. 'All gone.'

'All gone,' they said together.

Nic's phone pinged. That was Charlie on his way. He'd be here in a few hours.

Charlie accepted she'd bought the croft without consulting him in any way. He had had to, if he loved her. He understood that she had to have something that was totally hers before she became a we—even if that thing then became something they shared. The recent warning from the Crofting Commission wasn't a surprise.

Everything was taking five times longer than expected. They'd finally got the road finished, the sewage, water and electricity sorted, and their tiny but water-tight house built, and the larger, as-of-yet unheated workshop had walls and a roof. But he was still working on the ferry and she had a job in the local shop. And Nic's news yesterday. Another pregnancy was a lot, too much, every time, never a good time, yet he was hoping for a girl.

Why? He couldn't actually say. Was it the chance to see how he might raise a daughter? To help raise a daughter who would be just like her mother?

CHAPTER 17

Ben's whole body ached for the solitude and possibilities of deep water and, leaving his bags in the boot of his dad's car, he set out as soon as his dad parked at Grace's.

'Can I join you?' Sonny asked.

That was something Ben hadn't expected. His dad asking, after all these years. He stumbled ... 'I was going to really go for it.'

'I won't hold you back.'

The idea that he might just swim and swim out into the water without ever returning while his dad waited, worried, on the shore was a thought Ben liked. There was a cruelty there, not undeserved.

He looked over at his dad getting out of the car. He was unassuming but somehow assertive, like he'd made up his own mind and he'd push to come, even if Ben said no.

'Okay. But you may be sitting on the shore being eaten alive by midges.'

'I'll survive. I'll be just fine.'

'We have a few hours, right?'

'We should help cook and get ready,' Sonny said, but his face was looking to the path that would lead them to another and to the bigger loch.

'Everything is nearly ready, isn't it?'

'We have two hours. Max.'

Ben took a last look at his phone; it'd finally updated when he'd been in 4G. Nic had sent a few texts, including a video of Charlie walking with Star wrapped to him. He strode and sang. Then stopped so Nic could record a peaceful Star sleeping against his chest. Ben played it. Then replayed it for his dad.

'She has beautiful kids, I'll give her that.'

'And Charlie loves her.'

They were both silent at that, their loneliness an ache in the air around each of their bodies.

Ben pointed to his dad's feet. 'Those shoes will do. Spare swimming trunks in the boot by any chance?'

'No.'

'In the scud will be fine. No one is around.'

'Do you remember walking along a wild beach once, south of Edinburgh, when you were kids?'

'The one with the nudists that kept popping up among the dunes.'

'Like lemmings, their heads darting back and forth,

looking for like-minded folk.'

'That'll be us then. Something unexpected in the wild.' Up and through heather and bracken. 'Tick check later,' said Ben.

Sonny was thinking about the wee suckers finding the sweetest spots. He hated the blood-intimacy of the ticks, their silent imposition into private places, but he kept going. The path wound steeply through the wood, mixed with Scots pines and rowan and birch. Suddenly Ben stopped and Sonny nearly ran into the back of him.

'Whoah. Careful.'

To either side sloped the rocky face of a short, steep cliff. They were standing on an overhanging outcrop. Below them nestled the steep end of a sea loch.

'It was originally land-bound. An iceberg made it deep.' Ben thought of an overly dramatic sign he saw when walking in the Cairngorms, *A glacier died here*. 'But the sea broke through and it's brackish and gets saltier the further out you go.'

He stripped. He did have swimming trunks in his bag but he equalised the playing field by going in the buck like his dad would have to do.

'Don't hesitate or you'll think yourself out of it.'

'No chance.' And Sonny stripped down too.

Perhaps there was a similarity to the movement of their

torsos and their hips as they undressed, a shared darkness to their eyes. Maybe they occasionally made the same unconscious gestures of love and hopelessness. Ben took two steps back, then three forward, and launched himself out into the air over the water. Then gravity did its bit. He made a neat small splash, surfacing a bit further out. He glanced back, 'Come on old man.'

'Who you calling old? I'm not even middle-aged! 50 is the new 30.'

'Then why are you waiting? Are you scared?'

Ben turned and started to swim and was definitely not waiting for his dad. He did, however, look back as his dad swithered about jumping. The water was cold but he'd not say anything to put Sonny off as he looked down to assess the clearance. Then he looked out, rocked back on his heel, one step and another and he leapt. Ben imagined that in his head Sonny believed he was graceful, a linnet or hawk taking to flight rather than a cumbersome swan always finding it hard to free itself from the suction of the surface of the water. His willy swung and his arms flew out wide before they slapped down at his side on entry.

Sonny swam quickly to catch up and Ben found himself letting him. They moved through the water side by side, with less urgency than in years past, and as he pushed at his breath and stroke, with his dad beside him, Ben found his urge for the open sea diminishing. This was how we accept the pace of another.

Before they reached the mouth of the loch, both men turned and floated for a while in the sun.

'I'm off the rigs.'

'Good,' said Sonny.

The sun, the heat, no one else around.

'Does that explain your face?'

'Yes.' He noticed his dad's ease in the water. 'Do you ever swim when I'm not here?'

'Not really. It's something I associate with you.'

'Not with the place?'

'Not really.'

'You moving up here for good?' Ben asked.

'I am. It has felt, this time, like home.'

Ben wondered if he'd ever been the type of person to actually like travel, or his dad either. If his dad's parents had approved of Mum, if hers had of him, if other things were in place, would they not have settled here? And been happy?

Sonny started to swim again, but more slowly, and back towards shore. 'You go on, son, but I'm heading back.'

The sky to the north looked laden, a ways off, but moving this way.

'I'll come with you.' Ben had decided; he'd not swim out

today.

'Not for my sake.'

Ben thumbed towards the sky. 'That looks like a thunderhead.' Swimming side by side they headed not to the overhang but just a bit to the side, where they could walk out of the water.

Sonny let Ben pass and lead them up to the neat little pile of their clothes. There was generosity and apology, somehow, in how he opened his body as he turned towards Ben. They were both soaking wet and glistening in the sun.

'We'll be sore tomorrow,' Sonny said.

Ben knew they looked so much alike, were so much alike. He'd have to be the one to sort out how he felt about his mum and his dad and the job and his life, really. It didn't matter if he'd disappointed his dad. It wasn't his dad's situation to judge or to fix. Hell, he'd disappointed his kids enough, made mistakes, and even if he'd fought for family in the only way he knew how, which was to blindly take over when his wife absented herself, he'd certainly not made things easier on himself by refusing to let them dismiss Viv, to forget her altogether or to blame her for everything. "I wasn't easy to live with," Sonny had said only recently, but the possibility of an apology was undercut when he said, "but neither were you guys".

Still, there was a change in his dad and he'd been showing up more, brokering a peace with Nic in particular. She wasn't convinced but she also wasn't hostile to him. Perhaps today was Ben taking a first step towards his dad, seeing if he could change. If either of them were capable of it.

Nic and Charlie went down to the shore, with Star held close in the sling. Today, without their boy, they sat and as Nic fed Star, pleasure and fear tugged at her skin and deep behind her eyes. Charlie talked about his day captain and the comments he made about Charlie's potential. He was bright with the praise. It made sense. Charlie's ambition on the sea had been clear from the start. The croft, the kids: she'd been a fool.

She wished she had taken a nap; such a powerful exhaustion swept over her. She didn't rub her eyes or her heart but rather unbound her daughter and helped Charlie wrap himself up with her. Star slept and Nic imagined Finn was there with them: his hands playing with her hair and ears and always straining to look beyond her shoulders and swinging arms to the world. Inevitably he'd have grown tired and his head would be heavy against her back, his cheek indented by the contraptions of the straps of the pack, his other cheek exposed to the air, the wind, the adult laughter. She could almost feel the reassuring weight of Finn, even though today it was just her, Charlie and Star. She held Charlie's hand and they walked back to the house they'd built.

April helped Aly through the lunch crowd and with the lazy daytime drinkers. On her break April took Col down a quieter side street and they kissed like teenagers, almost forgetting where they were. Col left to go into Inverness to stock up for upcoming travels, and they arranged to meet at Grace's later.

April wondered when she'd tell Nic about Col. Whether tonight she'd introduce everyone and whether she and Nic might have time to talk, just the two of them, over the next few days. Nic would have her family around her—young and bound so tightly—creating a distraction and a silence they all fell into. She hadn't spoken of her worry about Nic's body, the headaches, how thin she'd become and how fast between pregnancies, her need, sometimes, for a drink, the wound-up nature of her and the blood vessels that sometimes raised at her temple when she ranted. How Nic threw her a certain hard look when she asked how she was.

And the accusation of it silenced April and a story would spill out about someone else at work, any job, any person: a funny drinker, a wanker boss—it didn't matter—or something Grace had done or some political rant. She could tell her about the near miss with Jason who she thought had real potential and then turned a bit scary over dinner talking about MI5 and the CIA and how to hide data. So much so that she'd had him drop her at Grace's place rather than her own, and Grace appeared and stood on the porch, having been woken by the car, her hands on her hips, cricket bat leaning against the door frame. Seemed to have been enough, for Mr Keen had not been into the bar again. So two boys, a near miss and now Col. Babies or no babies, husband or no husband, April would talk to Nic about the first night with Col, and then April would ask Nic about the croft, motherhood and how things were with Charlie and she'd listen to Nic talk.

Grace sat out on the decking with her neighbour Siobhan who'd been helping her cook. Grace placed an extravagant mid-afternoon G&T in front of each of them. The sun was high but a breeze kept it all a bit fresher. Siobhan kicked off her shoes; Grace had been barefoot all day. They talked gently about everyday things and Grace half-paid attention as she listened for an unfamiliar car approaching on the road, slowing, then stopping. She anticipated the perfume her sister always wore, the stride she had as she took no prisoners. Grace's hand gripped her glass. Siobhan reached over and put a hand on Grace's lower arm. 'Is there anything you want to talk about?' Grace found that there was.

CHAPTER 18

Spring Storm

Col sat at a table for two, alone, with a half-empty pint glass. A few women had flirted but Col wasn't interested. They were all legs and sparkle, and Col had chosen solitude over forced conversation. Beer sweat dampened the coaster and nervous fingers, not Col's, might later roll layers of the wet cardboard into a small ball and play with that.

The Still was a mid-sized village pub but it felt as if it could be lifted up in a strong wind, Dorothy style, and plopped down into the middle of moorland. The crowd here was unpretentious, friendly and varied. Col had not been for over a year, and had been stood up by a friend who had phoned to say her baby was sick and she couldn't make it. Col had already committed and so sat, alone. Predictably, an early spring storm had come in, and so the pub was warm with customers.

Today there were two bartenders. There was an old guy, Aly, who Col knew relatively well, who had earned the face ridges he wore. Col didn't think any of this bartender's life had been all that bad and yet much of it had contained strong Scottish winds and the burn of the sun — spend long enough out there and the sun hits you too.

And then there was April. She wore hiking boots, well-worn decent ones, and jeans which, when she came out from behind the bar to clear tables, could stand to be replaced or patched up. Her top, however, was newer, just a T-shirt with half-naked women on it and she'd used a marker to draw a red circle with a line through it. She could have worn the T-shirt ironically, but most people here would have missed the subtlety. Col wasn't sure which version of the shirt would have made her more attractive.

She'd tied a wool sweater, moss green, around her waist, and her dark hair was pulled back loosely in what some called 'swept up' into one of those half-ponytail half-buns. It looked like she put it up at the beginning of her shift and wouldn't touch it again. A thin cloth, one of those tacky touristy hand towels with puffins on it, hung from her waist and when she needed to she wiped her hands on it. She didn't care—hadn't ever cared what people thought.

April was a good bartender because she listened to people, poured even and fair measures, and didn't cheat her boss or the punters, and she kept a clean bar too. When bantering, she held her own with the witty locals who turned phrases with such ease, but between serving people Col saw that it was something she prepared herself for. This sociability, this ability to ease conversations between folk, was totally within her ken but not something she'd seek out. She served everyone in turn, except those who might need to be served first. The short ones, for instance, when it was busy and there was a heightened risk of a crush. And, sometimes, although she was careful with this, she'd serve the troublemakers who she wanted to clear away from the bar as quickly as possible.

Col hadn't seen her by-accident-on-purpose spill a drink on anyone but it seemed like that might be something she'd do. The regulars waited for a lull and simply raised a glass or a hand or their eyes and she served them easily and quickly and she tallied one or two tabs in her head or maybe on a piece of paper behind the bar and a few of them settled their scores at the end of the night. Only strangers got out of hand here and were quickly dealt with by a local who sat by the door most nights. Col knew Bob from time spent outside smoking. A good guy, big and gay, if Col was to guess. Guess, yes, but mention, no. In London or Glasgow, maybe. In a village outside Inverness, not so much.

Col had fierce beliefs and in younger, riskier days had been more hot-headed and vocal. Now, in a place like this, folk could think what they might, say what they might, and Col didn't offer, didn't correct. Sometimes this muting of opinions and self was exhausting.

Around nine, there was an open session. Clearly an opportunity for people who used to be in bands to get up and give it laldy for their friends. A friendly ruckus with impromptu dancing in the small spaces between tables, people pulling chairs and tables back to make room. There was talent here and it descended into a trad session that was a type of heaven. An urge to join in that took Col by surprise. A bodhran sat in the boot of the car, which Col brought out only rarely and with really good friends.

But in a room full of strangers Col thought, *Not who I am.* That's not a good thing to think, not at thirty, not at any age. We can always change, always do new things. Col waited at the bar, and was served last, once a space had opened up around them.

April asked Col's name and they chatted for a while. Small talk.

'Settle what you owe at the end, Col,' she said, and Col no longer felt like a stranger, was not yet a regular, but something familiar, and Col was happy enough with that. Col didn't, as they say, have a way with the ladies and was simply there trying not to fuck it up.

Once the band struck up again and the weather worsened

outside, barriers dropped, a couple from Poolewe squeezed into the table and there was banter and foot tapping and a few songs where everyone sang what they knew or clapped in appreciation for places the session took them that no one had expected.

'Who here has no way to get home?' the singer asked, as the windows rattled and a snow-filled dark swirled beyond the streetlights. A few tentative hands went up. Col was in a guest house around the corner and felt pretty confident about braving the short walk. April didn't raise her hand either.

'I'm suggesting a shut-in, Aly!'

Aly shrugged, non-committal. 'Those are illegal now, George, and you know it.'

'We'll see.'

But that night was a night everyone stayed until closing. It was impossible to leave, as if the music as well as the wind had pushed the door closed.

April seemed to know the band pretty well. She bore a passing resemblance to one guy who wasn't in the band but was clearly a best mate of the band. They both had dark hair and dark skin too, maybe just in this light or maybe everywhere. They were mixed race Col realised, on seeing her brother beside her. Her brother was big and confident and he had a way of asking for things from his sister that felt like an order, and Col thought he looked like a bit of an arsehole. But then. Her laughter, their easy familiar ways, how the brother collected the drinks from the bar, and a few for other tables too, when it got busy. Just everything. There was a fondness there and there was a changing of the mind, a softening to this big man, brother to this woman. Col's brother, Innis, was in New Zealand and if they'd ever had that ease it was long gone now and not to be reinstated.

The band was good but not great. In their patter they joked about it, working on the rigs, the stolen rehearsals, how many times they'd had to cancel gigs because bad weather meant they couldn't be where they were supposed to. They held up their empty pint glasses to Aly or April who'd laughed and raise a hand. 'Go on guys, you know it's okay. What's it to me.'

At some point, during a lull at the bar, April stood beside her brother with her hand on his shoulder, the night winding down. Col was nursing the last sips of the night's final beer, getting ready to push away from the table. April's brother tapped his hand quickly to his heart and then drew his sister towards the band.

'Liam, let's play us a song we can all sing to. April and I, something we know. "Green Grow the Rashes' or 'The Queen of Old Argyle", the brother suggested.

April tried to get back behind the bar but Aly and Hannah waved her away saying, 'We've got this. Why don't you give us a tune.'

'I want to hear this,' Hannah said, 'after all the humming you do around the place.'

The guy playing the mandolin handed it to her.

'What's this?' said the brother.

April accepted the mandolin and the chair. How it fit her hands, her body.

Turning to the band, she leaned in and said the name of a song. Her brother leaned in too and then took a step back shaking his head.

'I don't know that one.'

But she didn't hear or didn't listen and led them off, the band falling in, and she started to sing, half-facing the band as if singing just for them. It was a good sound, in this place; quiet though, as if private, and some people started to talk over her. Col lifted a hand to them, *Stop talking, please, can't you see what's happening here?* In the buzz of the room, no one paid attention to this small gesture of longing, and so Col had to make the effort to block out all the other noise and listen, strain to listen. Acceptance. Between the first note and the last and there was barely a glimmer of applause and Col couldn't understand it. She sang another, when Aly asked, one of her own. 'She's been singing this one in the stock room and it's lovely.'

And it was. A song of solitude and back-breaking work

and Col thought it was about finding a place in the world.

Col settled his bill while April was gathering in the praise after singing another duet with her brother and he nodded to her on the way out.

Col would hear her voice at odd times: driving home; walking an embankment looking at flood plains; looking for a water source; when doing nothing at all. Next time Col would strike up a conversation, would say something. Be noticed.

April watched Col leave and wondered why he hadn't waited. She'd have settled his bill for him. Let him sit there all night and watch her. Take him home with her?

What was it she felt? Alive. Seen. He saw it all and his gaze rested on her in the way favourite clothes make your body feel more awake and also totally at ease in the world. She noticed it because she had never before felt that in the company of anyone. Much less in a busy bar in which she found tonight she could notice no one else.

CHAPTER 19

The Brilliance of Light

It took Charlie a second, maybe two, to realise that Nic was failing to control their trajectory. Maybe there was a blur at the edge of the road, an animal dashing to safety, but his gaze skimmed past it to turn to Nic. In an instant he was remembering the dark circles under her eyes this morning, the unconscious movement of her hand through her hair, starting at her temple, soothing the nascent headache she hadn't yet named. He realised he'd noticed it and dismissed it in the same breath. But he saw it now, for a split second, from the backseat where he sat beside their daughter, and he reached for the wheel, too late.

Suddenly there were holes in what Nic could see. Brilliant absences. Adrenaline raced through her. She thought of picking chanterelles with Finn and of how he took her hand and led the way. Of her sister April lying injured on the ground after feeling the cold metal of the swing in her hand and how the summer heat raced to her palm when she let it go. The whisper of air upon her skin. The sound as the metal met the temple of her sister's head. And how what continued to confuse Nic was how she could never remember the full image of the scene. Perhaps, such strong emotions, such gaps.

Here on the road in her nippy little car she realised the danger too late. There was a shadow and blur where the road should be. She moved to avoid it and they were already within this breathlessness of blue as the ground below disappeared and they lived the speed and the shimmer; they were the shimmering and the suspension of light.

Maybe Nic slumped over the wheel. Maybe there was nothing in this world she could see.

Helen started at the noise of a car failing to take the bend. She swore and took a few steps towards the sound of the crash, but she knew better than to try to help, what with her knees and hips and her fingers that didn't bend or grasp as she'd need them to. She dialled 999 and then made her way to the crash site.

Ben's phone with its single bar rang and vibrated on Grace's kitchen table. No one heard it.

April's phone rang for the second time and this time she dug it out of her coat pocket.

'Hello, is this April Avens?'

'Yes. Who is this?'

'I'm Officer MacKay.'

'Excuse me?' April said, halting their walk, dropping Col's hand.

'I'm officer Pat MacKay and there's been an accident.'

The officer named a place, and although April didn't know it exactly she was thinking it was close to Nic and Charlie's croft, maybe.

'Who has been in an accident?'

'You're the third contact on Nicola Skirving's list.'

'It's Nic Avens-Skirving.'

'Excuse me, ma'am?'

'They're husband and wife, and did the double-barrel thing.'

'It says Skirving on the information I have here.'

'Why are you calling me? Where is Charlie? I assume he

was first on the list. What accident?'

'I'll try to take those questions one at a time. I'm calling you because there's been an accident on the B239. Your sister was in the car. So was Mr Skirving. And a baby.'

'Star. Her name is Star.'

'Star?' He paused.

April was thinking that the officer hadn't said next of kin. He hadn't said next of kin. 'How are they?'

'I'm afraid I can't say much else to you over the phone. But the air ambulance has taken the family to the hospital in Inverness.'

'Is it just the three of them?'

'Yes, Nicola and Charles and a little girl.'

'Okay. When did they leave?'

'They're expected to arrive at Raigmore at 5:20.'

'Please, can't you tell me if they're alive?'

'The adults are in critical condition.'

'What does that mean?'

'They were alive when the air ambulance took off.'

April shook her head.

'And the baby?'

The officer hesitated. 'The baby died on impact.'

'Oh my. Star.' She took a few steps forward, waved her

arm, filled her belly with breath. Exhaled. Choked. Col followed but slowly, kept a distance, and April felt that gentle action, noted it. Her sister and Charlie were riding in the air ambulance with their dead child. One of them had been driving.

'Ma'am.'

April's mind raced. There was no four-year-old.

'So there was no little boy in the car?'

'No, ma'am.'

She remembered. Finn was at nursery. Out for the day with his nursery class.

'Have you phoned anyone else?'

'As I said, you were third on the list.'

'Who was second?'

'Her brother, Ben.'

'And.'

'We couldn't get through.'

'Thank you officer. We will meet them at the hospital.'

April turned to Col: 'My sister has been in an accident,' and started to run to Grace's. 'I'll meet you there,' she said, hoping Col could choose the right paths. April dialled Grace's archaic landline as she ran via the most direct route.

Everyone was in the house milling about, putting things in bags, talking through options. Grace wouldn't let both kids get into the same car.

Grace stepped towards April. 'You go. Pick up Finn and bring him down. He's with his nursery teacher, right? No matter what happens he should be here.'

'Should he?'

'Yes,' said Grace.

'Okay. I know where to get him.'

'Ben, you stay here, with us.'

'It'd be better if we shared the driving,' he said.

'I won't have it,' said Sonny. 'I'll go with April.'

'Good,' Grace said.

'Are you sure, Dad? I can do it alone. I know the roads, it won't take long.'

April was thinking that people needed to be at the hospital for Nic, Charlie and Star. They need to handle any questions that came up.

'I'm sure,' her dad said and there was no negotiation in his voice.

'Drive carefully,' said Ben.

'Of course I will.'

'Of course, we will.'

'You guys too. Call us when you know anything. Anything.'

April was already out the door and Grace was only a few steps behind her, bag over her shoulder, car keys in hand. 'Come on, Ben.' But she needn't have said it for he was right behind her.

CHAPTER 20

On the way north towards the croft, her dad fidgeted and exhaled. He touched his face, rubbed his sweaty palms on his trousers and kept checking his phone. 'She'll be okay, right?'

'Dad, I don't know.' And she thought about how reserved the officer's responses had been and her loop of thought kept trying to catch onto what hadn't been said. 'We have a job to do and we do it. Other than that, we just have to be patient.'

'We'll need to a pack a bag for him.'

'Yes, I was going to go up to the house first.'

April filled the car with fuel in Ullapool, in that shocked, automatic way when crisis hits—just keep moving, have a small goal and reach it—and the woman behind the counter at the petrol station said to her, 'Have a good day.'

'You too,' April replied, with a nod, but she was thinking about Nic, Charlie and Star and she didn't meet the woman's eye.

As they got closer, she drove more slowly, particularly on one familiar curve. The road had been closed for a few hours but had just re-opened and so it was backed up with a queue of cars. She was forced to go slowly as the accident scene came up on the other side of the road. Fourteen orange bollards in a row, roughed up and scuffed with black from other instances of use, with blue and white POLICE ACCIDENT tape stretched taut between each one, and she knew they'd been erected only a few hours ago in this spot.

The bollards were arranged in a line where the guardrail was smashed through. The metal of the broken rail was twisted with the force of the car's momentum. Dark and muddy tracks marked the road where the car had been hooked and drawn up via a reverse path up out of the heather and bracken and onto a tow truck, which would take it to a garage so the damage could be assessed by the insurance company, maybe the police too. To determine fault or cause or both. No other car was involved.

Mud had fallen like cluster bombs onto the road and been flattened by the wheels of passing cars. April's car passed over the mud too. She wondered if in the days or weeks to come she or a family member might feel compelled to tie flowers to the barrier with a hand-written note that would soon be battered by the Scottish weather.

Her dad let out a long breath through gathered lips. The opposite of a sucking in. The ride had been nearly silent. They waited for a call from Grace or Ben with more information. There was nothing.

'That's good, right?' April asked.

'I hope so,' said Sonny. Not increasing but rather triggering April's concerns.

Half an hour or so later, they would be driving past again, heading south with Finn in the car, and she didn't know what to do. Should she draw attention to the cones and the disruption to the earth so he'd remember them in years to come? Should she encourage him to look in order to give him a memory he'd need to help make sense of today's happenings or should she distract him and have him look in the other direction? What would be better for him in ten or twenty years' time?

No matter what happened, either Charlie or Nic were driving and their daughter was now dead. Finn's sister was dead.

Ben and Grace went to the hospital in two cars, leaving five minutes apart. They took two cars in part so they'd have space to bring Nic and Charlie home, if they could. But since neither had called nor answered their phones, deep down they believed this would not be the case.

The signs to the parking garage were clear, but they were the last useful signs in the place. They met at the hospital entrance and half-ran like through a maze of stark corridors. Having no aversion to asking directions, they did so three times. And still. Miles of corridors, often of brick or white painted walls without any signage at all, with anonymous doors opening to the left or right, strangely unpeopled.

Finally, they arrived.

May Nic be alive. May Charlie be alive.

Maybe the woman behind the counter tried to break the news gently but that was not how it was received. Nic was dead.

Grace let out a gasped *No*, stumbled and caught herself on the counter of the nurses' station; righted herself, and her knees gave way. Ben stepped forward and caught her around the waist and also stumbled. With the clattering, the nurse came around the desk and led them to chairs. A few people got up so they could have chairs together. One woman brought little cups of water from the machine.

Grace cried contained tears, because that was her way, and Ben's body shook and he thought he could hear his bones rattle; if he were to open his eyes he would see without colour.

After a few minutes Grace stood, facing the nurse who was looking at a computer screen. 'And Charlie?' The nurse pressed her lips together, ran her finger along the edge of the screen, gathering facts, weighing up what she should say.

'He is in surgery. He'll be there all night, by the looks of it.'

And from the tone of her voice, the camber of her eyes, Grace knew that Charlie's life was at risk too.

April had sprinted away, and Col was immediately disorientated. Having been more than happy to follow, Col now found that the paths were labyrinthine, a mixture of forestry paths forged during felling, deer paths criss-crossing each other and somewhere, that was not at all obvious, were the human paths that smart people in the know, like April, could just race over towards their destination. Col walked slowly, trying to remember aspects of the landscape they'd passed through but as the hills curved and rose and dipped the vista changed so quickly. The markers noted on the way out were lost. The second time Col ended up back at April's cottage and not at Grace's, they descended the hill and went to Grace's via the road.

It had taken Col over an hour to get there and there was no movement within the house. The front door was locked but the backdoor was open. Col was unsure if Grace always left it that way or if it'd been left for Nic and Charlie who might come here because the phone call was a mistake and it had really been a different car, different lives in turmoil.

The house showed expectations of a day very different from the one that was transpiring. The downed branch prevented a BBQ and so food prep had moved inside and had been hastily abandoned. A frosted cake sat regally under a glass bonnet, and dishes and used utensils clattered in the sink as if the counters had been hastily cleared and as if, Col imagined, for the laying out of a body in death. It was a strange thing to imagine.

The house was in slight disarray and Col had the urge to make things right, to ease whatever the next few days would bring, and he gave into it, turning on the burners to finish the cooking, washing the dishes, drying them and finding their rightful spots in Grace's meticulously organised cabinets. Col went to the dresser and ran a hand along the old fiddle on a high shelf, picked up and weighed different stones in each hand, carefully replacing them back where they'd been found.

The gentle mess of the sitting room did not need to be shifted, and Col respected the necessary sense of the kitchen. Grace was a woman who wanted to know exactly where to go to get what she needed when she was cooking, so she could continue any conversation she was having as she made the food. Col could hear her easy laughter in both rooms but it was more present in the kitchen, and that was after only minutes of being in her company. Col would do right by her and by April. They may not eat, but Col seasoned the dishes and set out dishes and cutlery and glasses. Filling the kettle and setting out mugs, Col left by the back door, shutting it firmly and wishing the house, and those who would return to it, a gentle night.

CHAPTER 21

Cemeteries

Both cemeteries were comprised of small, sloped patches of ground that ended in cliffs that fell into the sea. One contained old family plots, of fathers and fathers of fathers and mothers and mothers of mothers and children dying at all ages, sometimes a falling list of names and dates that belied the loss and grief of each child taken too soon. This cemetery was a wind-pressed island home for the dead.

The other cemetery, on the mainland of Sutherland, just a few miles from the croft, was newer and cultivated beside an older collocation of headstones. Locals called it the incomer cemetery and this was where Nic and Star were buried.

The family wanted them put in the same coffin, but it wasn't allowed, and so their coffins, one adult and one infant, were buried in the same hand-dug hole with Star resting on Nic. Ben and April had insisted on digging the grave and lowering the coffins themselves. It wasn't the done way, these days, but it was a small, ineffectual gesture of love towards Nic.

Charlie's parents buried him on Lewis. Demanded it, although the Avens family asked them to reconsider many times. The undertaker was shocked that a family would split a husband and wife, especially those who had died so suddenly, so young, and with one of their children. Ben had to put his palms to his eyes sometimes to stop himself thinking about the distance between Nic, Star and Charlie, and what it would mean for Finn. It was a psychic distance as much as a physical one and on some days he could not bear what had been done to them.

When this disagreement first arose, an early morning meeting had been arranged by the lawyers, a type of mediation to encourage the two families to act with a bit more empathy, and the first thing Charlie's dad, John, said was, 'Would he really have wanted to be buried with the woman who killed him?'

And the Avenses countered, 'Would he really have wanted to be buried across the sea from his wife and daughter? Wouldn't it be right for Finn to be able to visit them all in one place?'

Siân, Charlie's mum, swayed just a bit at that. But her husband stomped his foot. 'No son of mine will be buried with the woman who killed him. Driving just like a woman. If he'd kept a firmer hand, they'd *all* still be alive.'

There was enormous restraint from the Avenses. Ben dug

his nails into his palm; Grace's hand on his shoulder was, in equal measure, a request for restraint and an encouragement for him to give into the sweet call and lay Charlie's dad flat with a quick left hook. They all had the urge but wouldn't give in, because it was exactly what these folks thought of them. Just because it was true, didn't make it true.

The Avenses walked out to the cars, knowing they'd failed Nic, Charlie and Star, as Charlie's parents remained entrenched in their hard-line stance.

'Did you see the way he looked at me?' Grace said, unlocking the car. 'And she actually moved her chair away.'

'I think they have issues with all of us.' He ran a finger across his cheek that held slightly darker hues than the average highlander.

'Islanders.'

'Right?'

Ben climbed into Grace's car beside her and let his thoughts have some airing, 'Wow. That man needs to develop some sort of filter.'

'I'd like to show him a firmer hand,' said Grace putting the car ungracefully through the gears and paces and taking them home. They drove in silence with Grace taking her fury out on the road and her car.

'Dad's right, you do ride the clutch.'

Grace pulled abruptly into a passing place. 'You can walk.'

'I mean, Grace, perfect driving. Your gear box will last forever.'

CHAPTER 22

Ben and Grace paced, checking in on Charlie every twenty minutes. Fussing. Grace knew she had a responsibility to Ben and put her arm around him like she had earlier in the day when everything had been different. He put his arm around her too. Who knew what they were thinking. It was a mess and a swirl in there. They had not called April and Sonny. It was agreed that this was not something you said over the phone; how could either of them drive after hearing this? This was not something you said in the abrupt, rude way the nurse had told them. She should have known better. This was not something you could hear. This was not something you could bear.

And then quickly it became something they could not withhold from Sonny and April, and Grace called Sonny and told him what he had a right to hear.

It was still light and there were a few hours before April would return and so Col turned a back on the road and headed into the hills, choosing the paths to follow on a whim, noting places returned to, stopping to watch the hills roll towards and away from each other and from Col, who was neither familiar nor stranger here. Unsure whether to head for Grace's or April's, Col went to Grace's to get the car and then checked into a B&B nearby. April would call when she could.

Finn came out of the teacher's house singing 'Ally Bally'. Sonny took Finn to the car and the teacher said to April, 'Sorry. I didn't know what else to do. I thought it best not to tell him. What could I say? The singing distracted me more than it did him.'

And so they picked up a bubbling, happy boy who nonetheless had questions. 'Where are mum and dad and Star?'

April held the door open and looked to her dad. He missed a beat but said, 'Their car stopped working and we've come to pick you up.' April noticed how her dad skirted along the edge of truth.

'Can't we go help them?'

'They're in good hands already. We might see them later— it depends on what happens.'

'You were going to sleep at my house anyway. We'll have

a fire, hot chocolate, stories under the stars.'

He gave her a shiny grin and started the song again as they buckled him into the car. April and Finn continued to sing and fairly quickly Sonny joined in. He had a good voice, and April couldn't remember ever hearing it before. Funny, at Hogmanay she remembered them having a go, but now looking back, her dad was watching, tapping his foot, taking photos, maybe?

April was doing the drive down too because when they went to make the switch, she saw Sonny's hands trembling. She held them in her own and said, 'I'll drive. It's okay. I've got this.'

Finn said politely, *Again, please*. Her throat parched with worry and thirst opened and her lungs rippled with how good the singing felt, the camaraderie with her nephew. She pitched the playlist, *Finn*, forward and onto 'Three Little Birds', a mother singing to her child—and they sang with Finn, gently, all of them losing themselves in the brilliant brightness that breath and song make in the throat and higher in the head and lower in the heart, losing herself here and glancing back at the shine of Finn's cheeks, chubby still, as he grinned and concentrated and sang. April noticed the police tape to the left and the long row of cones and the skid marks that cut into the heather and mud. A young female roe deer bounded through the field to the right and that's where she pointed, directing Finn's attention. Glanced might be a better word for she could not help looking left again; her voice faltered and she pressed the accelerator and then they were past.

There would be time to tell him about the bollards and Star. Time to tell him everything but now, more than anything, April wanted to transport Finn safely south to see his mother and father.

Having still heard nothing, Sonny suggested they stop and take a walk. 'A stretch of the legs would be good.'

When they opened the car door, Finn unfurled his fist to show Sonny a stone he'd found on the island they'd visited that day. Sonny traced the lines of the veins on his wrist across his palm (around the stone) and out alone each finger. Pinching each tip, like you might do with toes in this little piggy.

'Your hands are nothing like your mum's,' he said. 'Her hands are tougher and her fingers longer and thinner.'

Finn's were still rather stubby but good enough for holding on to, they decided. They walked for a while and Sonny hung back when his phone rang and Finn asked to be carried. April squatted down, he climbed onto her back, and he played with her hair as she carried him piggy-back.

'Your hair is nothing like mama's hair,' he said.

'No?'

'It's darker.'

'Or Daddy's.'

They walked a bit more with Finn sliding down and April having to scootch him up again.

'And you're not very good at piggy-backing.'

'Really?'

'Mama is better.'

'She's more graceful and taller.'

'Fatter.'

'No, Finn, I've got quite a bit of meat on my bones, naturally. Only when she was pregnant with Star.'

And he pinched her sides, then her cheeks, wrapping his arms around from behind.

'Okay. Okay. We're both chunky.'

He pressed his ear to her back.

'Laugh. Laugh like her.'

She manoeuvred and brought him around to the front and sat them both down on the ground. It was acrobatic and thrilling and there was a rush of joy to his cheeks. April tried to conjure a laugh, for Finn and for herself. She wondered what it would be like to have a recording of the people you loved, like you get recordings of bird song on 'what's that bird' apps. Different laughs and calls. This one would be 'adult fakes a laugh for a child'.

'Laugh,' Finn urged. Squeezing her sides.

April thought back to the time when she and Nic were watching videos of some rough ferry crossings, with tables and chairs sliding-flying one way and then another across the bar area and then back with the other side of the swell. In the background you could hear crockery and glasses shattering.

'It wasn't funny,' Nic had said when one video came on. 'I was back there. If CSI cared about crockery, that's a scene they'd use in their trailer.' But they'd watched and Nic's laugh was unmistakeable. 'That was the glasses from the bar smashing,' she said. 'It was a mess.' And she hit replay—the comical tumble of tables and chairs, the precarious footing of the barman—and the sisters had let loose.

April tried hard to imitate it.

Finn looked up towards her lips, to try to see if her mouth looked like his mum's mouth when she laughed, and said, 'Try again.'

April thought of flying chairs and tables and plates and pint glasses, her shoulders moving back and her neck lengthening. Her body filled with laughter.

He giggled. Finn put one hand to her belly that jiggled and rumbled with the laugh. He clasped one hand over his mouth, trying to hold it in, saw his mum in his aunt. He liked April's laugh too.

'I'm thinking about your mum out on the ferry deck exchanging vows with your dad while it was blowing a hoolie.'

'I was there too,' Finn said pointing to his belly, which he made round by letting it fill with air.

'Yes, you were there.' They both placed their hands on their bellies like Santa did and they laughed.

'Sweetheart,' she heard her dad say quietly and she wouldn't remember hearing anything else. She wouldn't know if she let Finn run wild or if the earth stopped turning or if she drove or her dad did. It was the end of sense, for a while.

CHAPTER 23

Unmagical Thinking

Some call the siege of shock and grief 'magical thinking', but Sonny did not experience it as thinking, or as magical, but felt it in his breast bone, like a burn with a sharp, red-hot poker and it wasn't a flight of the imagination, it was persistently real; April's heart raced and blood pounded through her, giving her no rest (let's not talk about the tears that were often, unexpectedly overwhelming, or the pains she had in her body that had no discernible cause but this); Ben's breath caught and thick pressure built behind his eyes and an anger spread across his chest; a soaring sorrow in Grace had none of the sweetness that had been present when Suzie had died, a grief full of love for someone who had lived a full life, instead what she carried with her every minute of every day since knowing Nic, Star and Charlie were dead was the knowledge that she could not give in to the emotions she had because if she did she may never move again.

CHAPTER 24

Blindspot

The young police officer was overly direct, sitting there in Grace's living room. The Avenses encircled him but he deflected any sense of being trapped by firing questions off like bullets. Grace had made him a cup of tea with milk and sugar, which to her thinking (which she knew might be wrong thinking), was the way a child took tea and in fact the officer didn't look like he'd long left school.

'Did she drink much? Ever during the day?'

'Did she have a habit of driving too fast?'

'Did she have any medical conditions?'

'No. No. Not usually. No—she'd recently had a baby.'

Eyes widened with a new thought, above a crisp uniform. 'Was she suffering from post-partum depression?'

This implied, this question implied, that she was not in her right mind, that she was hormone-addled and caused the crash.

'No,' they said, although none of them knew for sure.

'Did she have any issues with anger?'

'No.'

'But we do,' said Ben. A statement, maybe a bit of a warning, or even a threat. And his father and aunt wanted to say, yes, really he does, in particular.

The officer did not take a step back, but readjusted. Had forgotten. 'I'm not intending to imply—'

'But you are implying. You're digging. You're accusing. That's what you are doing.'

'These are standard questions.'

'Being asked of people who weren't at the scene. What can we tell you about it?'

'You knew her and she was driving and three people have died.'

'Including her: Nic, my daughter.' Sonny leaned forward, his hand on his knee, shoulders squared.

'That's why we're asking questions about her mental state.'

'Have you checked the car, the brakes, for faults? Have you checked for animal tracks—deer, hares, anything. It can be like trying to drive through a safari park sometimes, up there.'

'And so she should have been driving slower.'

'You know how fast she was driving?'

The officer flustered. 'Not exactly. We have a witness, though who said she was going at a "neat clip".'

'What the fuck does that mean?' Grace asked.

'She was speeding,' the officer clarified. April was ready to hold Ben back. Sonny was beside Grace with a hand on her shoulder for the same reason. This was Grace who was usually the height of calm.

Grace shook herself free and stepped forward. Took the officer gently by the arm and led him across the room and out of the door. 'So, new to this job are we?' She was patronising. The family knew that grip on the arm, the steady firm direction—Grace could take you where she wanted to take you, whether you wanted to go or not. She handled both the officer and the opening and closing of the doors. As they walked down the slope of grass to the road she continued, 'If your goal was to mix a good more anger into our grief, you have succeeded. You've been a distraction, but not a good one. She is our family.'

'Was,' the officer said.

'Really? There must be some sort of training you can go on.' Grace continued to guide the officer down the path and to the waiting patrol car. 'Nic is our family. We were not there at the crash. No information we can give you can be of help to you. Expect some contact from your senior officer about a complaint and an order for you to go on sensitivity training.'

It was only later that the question about Nic's health struck April as pertinent. She was thinking about the few times she'd had migraines, along with the vomiting, and how she'd told Nic the story of when she got fired from the housing office job and how she had to stop the car half a dozen times on her way home to lose her guts. Nic responded, said, 'Sometimes my vision goes, I'm tired or excited or stressed or some combination of all of them and the world shimmers briefly and then goes blank in spots. There are holes.'

'Since when?'

'Oh, it doesn't matter. I sleep it off and it's fine when I wake.'

April let it drop and she'd be lying if she said she knew something was wrong, because it wasn't the truth. Nic told them very little. She could have had post-partum depression, she could have been drinking in the daytime, she could have had headaches that took her vision from her, but how were they to know, because she never told them. Because they weren't there enough. Because they didn't ask her often enough and hadn't pressed her. They didn't ask because as a family they had the habit of keeping everything on the surface in order to keep the family ticking over.

She didn't tell the officer, but she did tell Grace and Ben, and later her dad. Each of them exhaled as if a piece of the puzzle had fallen into place.

CHAPTER 25

The doctor had sad eyes to begin with and he didn't make any promises about the outcome of the surgery and so no one made any promises to anyone.

'Go home. Charlie will not be out of surgery before morning. If there's news we will call you. You're not next of kin but we understand the situation. Go home.'

And so, in their two cars, five minutes apart, they drove slowly and carefully to Grace's.

On the road below Grace's they met April and Sonny and Finn. The adults, in turn, greeted Finn, lifted him up, and held him tight. Put a smile on their face and said, *How is our Finn doing?*

Grace took Finn's hand and led them all up to her house, which was waiting for them. This is what they knew now: Star died on impact. Nic died in the air ambulance. Almost as soon as they hit the air.

Ben wanted to believe they'd put Star in Nic's arms as the familiar ground grew distant below.

Finn held Grace's hand and squeezed it. She squeezed back and lifted him, breathing in the smell of the sea and heather and the earthy smell Nic had had since she started gardening, and her son had carried it to Grace who glanced back at April. The girl had come so far; may this not be something to unbridle her doubts again. April thought of the road, the tyre tracks that led through the heather, and meeting Ben at the brow of the hill in the snowstorm and the swirl of it all. Ben thought of Nic and how she'd placed Finn in his arms for the first time and said she trusted him. Sonny let himself think about Star's ridiculous, perfect name and his daughter who'd name her child such a thing.

How do we do we grieve?

How do we do we grieve again? Grace wondered, thinking of other absences, other deaths. *We do this differently. We must do this differently.*

The cottage windows were cracked open to dispel the heat, and beneath the fresh evening air lingered the spices of dinner. No one but Grace really noticed the differences Col's interventions made to the house. They hadn't noticed the fluster of the place before they'd left and they didn't see the order now. Grace noted the thoughtfulness of it all and that Col understood welcome: you make the invitation, even though it may not be taken up. *Remember to eat and take care of yourselves, this could be a long night.—Col*

Ben played with Finn in the yard, gently, for a little while, as he climbed over and back over the fallen tree limb, picking off smaller branches and loving how they bent rather than cracked.

There was a question of what they could do for Charlie. They'd left the hospital as they'd been advised but there was a sense of that not being right, of Charlie being left on his own, even if he was in surgery. The police had called Charlie's mother, but it was too late for his parents to get to the mainland. The first ferry left at 6am and they could be at the hospital by ten at the earliest.

Please let him live until then, and many years past.

Grace called Charlie's mum, Siân, and they were struggling to find the right words. Sonny flustered beside her not knowing what to do with his hands. At one point April thought he was going to drape himself over Grace, so she could hold him up. Then the urge appeared to pass and he stood straight and held Grace's elbow. Her hand held the phone lightly, away from her ears. It was too much to bear.

Abruptly Siân asked who was driving.

'We don't know who was driving.' Grace said.

'It was her,' Siân said. 'John always says she drives like a rally driver.'

'We don't know yet,' Grace repeated.

Down the phone Siân made a sound—grief, blame—it was hard to say.

Finally she asked after Finn.

'He's good,' Grace said. 'He loves hanging out with April and Ben. They're great with him. April and Sonny drove up tonight to bring him down here.'

Grace nodded, listening, backtracking on any note of optimism or salvage. 'Yes, yes, of course, he's doing well despite everything. No, no, he doesn't know. Not yet. We thought we'd wait until we knew about Charlie.' Grace put the phone on the counter and put it on speaker. Siân went silent at the other end of the phone. Grace asked if her husband was there to support her.

'No, no. He's out.'

'Do you need help contacting him?'

'There's no need. Don't you worry, that's my business. We can talk tomorrow about Finn coming back to the island with us.'

'Well, Siân, that's jumping the gun. Finn is quite safe here, for now. No need to rush him to an unfamiliar island.'

Sonny was stunned, silently, his mouth opening to rage, they could all tell, and Grace covered the phone before he connected his urge to lay into them with his vocal chords.

'They've visited many times. Finn loves it here. I'm his gran. It's the best place for him while Charlie recovers. They'll both need a stable household. Which of you might be able to look after him?'

'We don't know what has happened. Or what tomorrow will bring.'

Siân hadn't seen the doctor's eyes. She couldn't know the clawing certainty that they would lose Charlie too. 'We'll let you know if we hear. When we hear. We hope you will do the same. Travel safely, Siân. We'll see you tomorrow then.'

Sonny mimed the action of putting on boxing gloves. Grace put the phone onto the charger and smoothed her jumper, then her hair.

'Really, Sonny. That's what you're thinking about tonight? With Nic and Star dead? That woman's husband can't even be bothered to come home to support her with news like this and you are ready to punch her? I mean, Charlie didn't say much but when he did, he never had a good word to say about his father, but still. She wants to believe she can do something for someone. In this case it's Finn. The promise of some action that might just save her son or help her grandson. I bet that's what she's thinking.' Sonny looked at Grace. She was right, of course.

'I'm mean she's off her head if we're going to let her take him to some godforsaken island to live with her and an abusive alcoholic.'

'Grace. You don't know that.'

'That's true. But there's understanding and then there's stupidity.'

Knowing it was important to eat something but not having much zest for it, the Avenses sat and picked at the food. After a time, April and Grace did the dishes side by side, Grace scraping the uneaten food into the compost and then washing the plates, and April drying. The window above the sink looked out over the road. They watched a car drive past, turn around and make a second, slower, pass. This time, with the late-evening sun clear on her face, they saw it was Viv. What she'd see from her car was Sonny and Ben with Finn in the living room and April and Grace at the window standing side by side. April placed her hand on Grace's forearm as Grace still had both hands shoved into the dishwater. They looked to the road, met the gaze of the driver and neither made any move to welcome her in.

The car moved slowly on and made no return.

CHAPTER 26

The Croft

The Avens family were to find out that a married couple dying suddenly at the same time, without a will, was a tricky area of the law. The funerals and burials had been the first contested area, which they'd had to concede. Custody of Finn came next and was tied up with questions of the tenancy of the croft.

The Avenses would not play well in court if it went that far, was what their lawyer told them. She was young, casually dressed, with a number of relatively neat piles of papers and folders, many of them colour-coded, on her desk, to show she was in demand but on top of it all. There were a number of areas of concern for her.

'Viv's departure and continued absence is … unfortunate.'

April sat forward; Ben stiffened. 'It's for the best,' they said together.

She nodded, 'I know. That's clear. I'm talking about possible perceptions, which can be different from reality. Beyond that there's the fighting, as in punch-ups, that seemed to be endemic in the family.' She looked at Ben and at April.

Well, when she put it like that. Yes, maybe not ideal.

'That YouTube footage of April's pub brawl in Glasgow is quite something.'

She seemed overly familiar, but the Avenses found that, despite her blunt character assessments, they liked her. There'd be no beating around the bush.

'And then there's you, Sonny,' she said pointing at him, 'taking your family to dangerous places, a rocky marriage, the nature of the work you do,' here she paused, waiting to see if Sonny responded.

'The work I used to do,' he said. 'I work with cars now.'

She nodded. 'And you tried to raise the kids alone, but there could be questions about the quality of their upbringing. How does that speak to consistency of the home life you could give to your grandchild?'

Blunt. 'I worked, I took care of them, they're still here.'

Nic was not there. His error was loud in the room.

The lawyer broke through it. 'You're a single man living in temporary accommodation, partially and, in my opinion, under-employed, and so that speaks to nuclear family or what version of it you might be able to provide.'

Despite the grit in Sonny's throat and at the outer edges

of his eyes, which he took to be a precursor to a rant, he brought them back on track. 'So they want Finn.'

'Yes. Full custody.'

'And you think they'll win.'

'I do. Ben is unemployed, April works part-time in a pub, Grace is in her second year of running a small business, which is quite a precarious venture, and you we've covered. The courts will be looking for stability and it's lacking. So yes, I think they'll win.'

'Well, that's not good enough. What are our options?'

'We'll get to that. From what I've been able to gather, they don't even want you to have visitation rights. They say you're bad influences.' She looked between the kids. 'They want to argue that the influence of your sister-in-law Grace would be negative upon Finn.'

'What does that mean?' April asked. Grace gave a small smile that said, bring it on.

'This is one we'd win. The laws are clear in this instance, and any arbiter should be very firm about that.'

So, Grace aside, looked at in these terms, they were all doing pretty badly at living a good, moral life, according to the laws of the land. There seemed to be the real world that was messy and interesting and then there was what would 'play well in court'.

'We need to put our terms forward. We want shared

custody of Finn. And if they get him, we have to have visitation rights. That has to be non-negotiable,' said Ben.

'You may not be in a position to negotiate.'

'And the croft?'

'In theory they can't touch that since it's in Nic's name. Although they're arguing that it passed to Charlie, because he lived longer than Nic and so it should be his, and they should be able to do what they want with it. I don't think the executor will go for it, but it's their argument and I thought you should know.'

'He outlived her by fourteen hours. And he was never conscious. That's ridiculous.'

'I had a look at the Crofting Commission's website,' Ben said. 'Shouldn't it pass to Finn? Tenancy is often inter-generational, right?'

'Yes, it is. But you never know. And they want to sell it, they're saying.'

Ben stood up, slammed his hands on the desk. 'They will not get their hands on Nic's tenancy. She fought for it and it was hers. It's Finn's and they have no right to take it from him.'

'They're firm that he'll grow up on the Island with his family.'

'What does that mean? We're his family.'

'They believe he should take after his father and

grandfather.'

'What does that mean? From what I can tell Charlie wasn't very much like his father at all, and that was a very good thing.'

'They both worked at sea.'

'The similarity ends there,' Ben said. 'He didn't know his father for his first four years and when he came back that house was not a happy one.'

'Rein it in, Ben,' Sonny said.

This lawyer was unflappable, it would seem.

'Who knows what a child will become? How can anyone know this? Finn needs both sides of the family, he needs to know he can return to the only place he'll really remember seeing his parents.'

'A guardian will need to be appointed for Finn.'

'I'm his godfather,' Ben said, and the rest of his family turned to him. News to them.

'There's nothing here indicating that.'

'Nic asked me and I said yes.'

'Do you have a date of the ceremony?'

'There was no ceremony. It was simply agreed. I have some text messages, maybe. Finn is my responsibility.'

'No ceremony, no papers, no proof.'

'Are the Skirvings paying you to be this negative?'

'We can't go on hearsay. We need facts.' She moved a few papers around. 'The good news is …'

'There's good news?' Sonny asked. 'Couldn't you have started with that?'

She ignored him. 'Until it's been decided in court, they try to change as little as possible for the child. If someone in the family is willing to look after the croft and be temporary guardian for Finn, the court would look favourably on them.'

They looked to April, which she didn't understand. Because she's a girl? She loved Finn, of course, but the croft wasn't for her. She didn't want that responsibility. 'I'm not the right person, Ben is.'

A clock ticked somewhere. Heads turned from April to Ben. The lines of his face smoothed as he considered this.

'I agree,' Grace said.

'Me, too,' said Sonny.

Ben looked at the lawyer. 'I'm the right person to raise Finn,' he said. 'It's what Nic and Charlie would have wanted. I know it.'

Ben was single, had recently been fired from the rigs for fighting and was currently unemployed, but the family had decided, together.

'Great,' said the lawyer with the small smile of someone

who likes a challenge. 'I'll take that to them.'

Ben left the lawyer's office and drove north to the croft. A few days after Charlie died, he and April had done the same thing but only been there for a few minutes, looking for legal documents, and no one had been there since. What do you do with the things that belong to people who had no intention of leaving this world? How do you go through your sister's things? Things she never intended you to see?

How are you supposed to use the things of a dead person, if you live in their house? A house you never expected to live in? How do you make it a home for a four-year-old who has only ever known this to be a house he shared with his parents? How do you step in and parent a four-year-old who's just lost both parents?

Siân Skirving was sitting in her car outside Charlie's house. She'd been here for some time building up the nerve to go in.

Much to her shame, she'd only been to the croft once before now when Finn had just been born. She and Nic had gotten on well enough then—Siân recognised the new-mother dwam, the overwhelming love and worry, and knew that where she was, how far from anyone, with a husband at sea, would add to that. Isolation brings its own exhaustion. The house had barely been completed and they had only the bare bones of furniture then and she'd shown such disdain about their choices. There was good croft land on Lewis and that was a better place to raise a family. She'd felt slighted—still did, deep down—that Charlie hadn't chosen to live near her.

What would the house be like now? Siân didn't really feel she had the right to go in.

A car made its way along the road, throwing up dust. She sat up taller, checked her hair in the rear-view mirror, took a deep breath and stepped out of the car to greet Ben.

She found herself talking about the weather. It was a kind introduction to this unexpected meeting, both being caught doing something they shouldn't, quite, be doing. No worries, no disagreement. They didn't know exactly why they were here or what they could do but they were now in it together.

Ben fetched the key from under a rock that was, in an ironic fashion, marked with an X (so much like Nic, thought Ben; so much like Charlie, thought Siân), and opened the door. He let Siân walk through first and she had the distinct feeling that he stood close to her in case she should falter. She felt she could do the same, that he could put his hand on her shoulder to steady himself. They both needed to work hard not to give into the flights of thought that had been so dangerous. She didn't know where to start, how to do what she was thinking of doing. What was okay for her to do?

Legally they couldn't remove or take anything of value. Should they box things up? Get it ready for a move, for someone else to live here?

Quietly, they started to move around each other around the house. Seeing a task that could be done and attending to it: slotting books onto shelves, organising magazines into piles, doing the dishes, and the laundry that was in the basket. Putting away what was hanging on the pulley.

It was a nice enough day with a good wind and so together they put up the line outside and hung the clothes and then the sheets they'd stripped from the beds and washed.

They had regular tea breaks. Siân was good company, direct, a talker. It wasn't what Ben expected of her. Ben made them a mushroom omelette and toast for lunch and they sat at the table side by side, looking out towards the sea.

'I left John in the guest house. Sleeping it off. He'll be furious. He's a mile from town without a car.'

Ben was thinking he was one you had to handle, a bit like his mother, but harder, even. It was a useful thought, that scale of difficulty, and he struggled for words to fill the space that didn't sound judgmental or patronising.

She charged forward: 'I think I'm going to leave him. Can you believe it's something I've never thought about until Charlie died? Never once. Even thinking it makes me feel a bit giddy.'

'It's a big decision after such a shock.'

'Isn't that exactly why we make big decisions? I only have this one life.'

Together they made the beds and boxed up some clothes to give to charity. At one point, they met in the hall, each with a small box in their hands, *Can I take this?* Neither asked what it was the other wanted by way of memorial but the boxes, small and fitting into the palm, for Siân, and more rectangular, for Charlie, made it into Siân's handbag and onto the passenger seat of Ben's car.

Siân made chicken, potatoes and salad for dinner, and they stayed up talking for quite some time. Nic and Charlie were there in their talk, of course; they were everywhere in the house. But they shared a bottle of wine, then part of another, and talked about themselves. Siân about her childhood in Oban, about how handsome John had been, and charming. And how that charm soon faded. How he was gone more than home, especially when Charlie was young. He hated young kids.

'Then why would he fight for Finn?'

'It's the idea of bloodlines. It's the fact that his family line is weak; Finn is the only grandchild and he wanted him to have an island heritage.'

Ben noted the past tense, not quite willing to have hope that something was changing in her mind.

'But it's a lie. There, I've said it. He doesn't like your family, and so anything that's a dig to you he'll go for.'

She asked about Ben's tattoos when he had his sleeves rolled up doing the dishes. Siân was drying. He talked about the rigs, and she said that the culture of it sounded like the same as on the boats.

'I'll admit it was great at first. I showed up, did the work, the guys were often hilarious, freed of domestic responsibilities, their family photos next to their bunk beds, which we shared, in shifts. But I quickly realised it wasn't for me. It was empty. Full of exaggeration, of swagger and challenge and talk of girlfriends who were mistresses like that's normal, and let's not get started on the porn.'

Siân tapped his arm, 'So, what about these?'

And then Ben surprised himself by talking about the fight with his mother to a woman who could use it against them.

'How old were you?'

'Fourteen.'

'And Viv, your mother, an adult, hit you, a child, back?'

'When you put it like that.'

'That's the way you should put it.'

'It wasn't exactly like that. She threatened to send me away to school so I could learn some discipline. Said she couldn't do anything with me. She'd filled in an application and everything—it was sitting on the counter, in a stamped addressed envelope. Said nothing I could do would change her mind. I wanted to hurt her, and I was as big as she was—she was right to hit me back. It was self-defence. I'm responsible for her leaving.'

'You wanted her to behave better. To be the parent and help you behave better.'

Ben didn't say anything.

'She's responsible for leaving. End of story.' Siân paused, making sure he had taken it in. Then she continued, 'Does she know Nic's dead?'

Ben shook his head. 'I don't know what she knows of any of us. None of us is really in touch with her.'

'That's better for you. It's also better she doesn't know about Nic. It's hard to lose a child. It'd take a certain frame of mind to survive it.'

The air grew thick. 'Charlie was your only son. This must be devastating. I still have April and my folks and Grace.'

'I have John.' She laughed and so did Ben. Siân pointed to

his arm once more: 'But why the marks?'

'My days are numbered, and I actively contributed to that. Doing a job I hated and each flight to and from the rigs aged me.'

Siân nodded. 'So they're marks of your inaction.'

'You could say that, yes. Reminders.'

'I have a few of my own.' She showed him a teeth-shaped scar on her upper arm, a burn on her back. 'He threw a pot of pasta at me as I left the room.' And defensive wounds on her arms. From 'a neat little blade' he always carried with him.

Ben refilled their glasses and the sun glinted off the windows of the workshop.

'What were they going to make in there?'

'Nic wanted to make bespoke tools.'

'That sounds fidgety.'

'It is, but it suited her. To make something that would help someone to make something else.'

Siân talked about the furniture she made when John was away at sea. Some repairs of items in the house, and then a few new small pieces like a side tables, bookshelves, and a stool.

Ben said he'd always wanted to be a maths teacher. 'I hated maths at school but that's how it was taught. But I'm good at it and that's what got me through. They teach it so badly. I think you could make it more exciting, show kids how it matters in the real world.'

'I loved maths too. But the teacher told me girls can't do maths.'

'And boys couldn't do home economics.'

'I've never been one for cleaning and cooking, but John is an unreformed chauvinist and doesn't lift a finger. I do it all.'

'I never dust, but quite like vacuuming and having clean sheets.'

'On that note. To bed.'

They found a wine saver and suctioned the air out of the second bottle for one of them to take home with them.

'I'll take the guest room,' Siân said.

That left Ben with Finn's bed or Charlie's and Nic's. He thought he had to be brave.

They stood by their respective doors. 'Good night, Siân.'

'An unexpected pleasure.'

They both liked their coffee strong—one cup before moving onto tea for the day—and their porridge with a pinch of salt and a sprinkling of sugar.

They worked out a plan, sitting across the table. Siân was easy to be with and work beside. It was a natural solution, which you couldn't predict until two people in grief travelled to the house of the loved ones they had lost just to keep their hands busy and because they knew a child needed a home and someone needed to make it ready. The same urge.

'We're agreed.'

'Do we ask everyone?'

'We check with the lawyers; quietly first, and then we tell people. No negotiation.'

They agreed that Ben would take responsibility for the housework and school runs. Siân had had enough of that for a lifetime. She'd do her share, sure, and she'd keep the accounts for the house and croft. They'd both find work and find something to do on the croft that satisfied the Crofting Commission. They'd split the tasks so that they each had an even share of responsibility for making sure it ran smoothly.

'I'm pleased you were here,' said Ben, giving her a big smile and feeling the hope of this place being pressed between the sea and the moors; the last day a bridge between the past and future. The wind off the sea made his cheeks red. His coat was on the backseat of the car and goose pimples came up on his arm.

'I'll be seeing you soon.'

'Back here for when Finn starts school.'

'If not before.'

Their hug was light and full of love already.

'It's a good plan, right?'

'It's bonkers. But a great plan, for now.'

'For now.'

'Good luck with John. Call if you need backup.'

'Oh, I'm not going back to where he is. Don't you worry. I'll only be meeting John with our lawyers present.'

They exchanged phone numbers. Siân left first and Ben walked down to the water so he'd not be following her all the way along the road south.

CHAPTER 27

And still, grief

Ben allowed his skin to grow thin and he did not shy away from anything that came up and it made him stronger, he was sure of it, and for the first time in years he could think about his mother without fury but could not think of Nic without a shock hitting him and he never wanted to lose that, never wanted that to lessen.

Searing pain ran all along and underneath April's right shoulder blade, from splitting wood, from hauling plates back and forth to the pub's kitchen, from grief. Still. April called them ugly tears and Col said, *Bring them on.* April didn't want to get out of bed, and Col opened the window and let the world in. *Just a quick walk?* And sometimes she could only manage a few minutes. Once they were fifteen minutes away and she thought her appendix had burst with the pain she felt, that doubled her over, but it was only grief. Col travelled for work and always came back. Grace visited and Ben visited and they all drank and went for walks or swam, depending on the season. Her dad was around but awkward and

April didn't have the energy to fix whatever was broken between them and she hoped, foolishly, that it'd fix itself. Col reminded her to breathe. Ben reminded her that her life was a hell of a lot more stable than his own and that she didn't have a four-year-old to care for. It eased. Loving made the grief sharper, sweeter, better. It eased. Made a sudden, short, shock return. Eased.

Grace had never known a grief like this. It weighed her down and so Grace started to give away things that had been in the dresser for years: a tea set to Siobhan and the boardgames to Ben, the mandolin to April. She was thinking that recipes only come alive when made with our hands, and only made brilliant when shared with others, and so too these objects of memory. She had two collections of stones. One pile were stones she'd picked up on walks she'd taken with April, Finn and Sonny—and these she gave back to the forest, one at a time, holding that person in her thoughts for the day, making their favourite cake, which she'd then eat and share with whoever might show up. The second cluster were stones she'd gathered with Nic that first trip to the croft, so she headed north and with Ben and Finn beside her she surrendered each stone back to Nic's land.

At other times she did not believe Nic was dead, not really. She'd seen the body and it wasn't like she believed Nic was a ghost, but more that she didn't feel her death or her absence. But at the classic times when everyone else wept (like upon hearing the news; at the funeral; on the first anniversary), she was calm and terrifyingly present, practical and unmoved. So for quite some time after Nic had died there were still times that Grace could not acknowledge Nic was gone because to do so would be unbearable. It would break her.

Grief worked in Sonny as a force that moved tectonic plates. The resulting quake was unexpected. In grief for his daughter he realised his grief for his relationship with his son and his marriage; he realised he was also a grief-maker. When working abroad he'd repaired all sorts of things, but it was the weapons that bothered Sonny. There was no point at which the weapons he was responsible for did not bring grief upon others. He did not pull the trigger but he'd made sure the trigger worked. With his family there was little he could do right and he'd been responsible for inattention and inaction and sadness and resentment. They tolerated him but didn't trust him. They were right in this. Nic's last email was simply a link to a podcast about toxic masculinity. Whatever he thought about being a father and a man didn't fit in this century. He didn't know how to bring himself up to date. He still wanted things for his other kids but they seemed to be the opposite of what they wanted for themselves. And so he held tight. He showed up. He tried to ask questions and listen to the responses. He still wanted to get in touch with Viv; he thought it's what they should do, felt it was morally wrong to keep Nic's death from her. But reluctantly he listened to his children; finally he let them make this decision about their own lives.

During that first summer Finn lived at Grace's. He asked after his mum and dad and sister almost every day and they all gave him steady, sure answers and let him know how much they loved him.

Once or twice, Finn lashed out and demanded to see his parents. 'Go get them, bring them here and let them take me home,' he'd say. He knew his parents and sister were dead, why he was at Grace's, and that the plan was for him to go home with Ben and Siân soon. He settled when they talked about the croft and so that's how they calmed him—talking about the croft, the house, and the sea.

When they arrived at the croft house almost two months after the crash, he raced up to the door and April and Ben were close behind. April understood, suddenly, desperately, that, despite being told otherwise, Finn believed his mum, dad and sister would be there. Part of her hoped it too. That they were all wrong and Nic and Charlie had just been on holiday and playing a practical joke on all of them. While Ben put the key in the lock,

April stood behind Finn with him leaning back against her legs, her hand running through his hair.

'They're not here Finn,' April whispered into his hair, but when the door opened he ran ahead and into every room. He didn't shout out but it was clear what he was looking for.

They stood for a few minutes until Ben sought Finn out and found him in his parent's room unable to move. Ben lifted him into his arms. They were crying when they came back into the room. April too.

They understood that his hope was really a need; one that would go unfulfilled.

Later that day Siân arrived and they all watched as she quietly, unobtrusively checked all the rooms too, just in case.

The island light always had the sea in it. Sutherland light was anchored by land and by family. Siân preferred Sutherland. They could see the ferry from the croft and it marked her days. She missed Charlie, but his death had allowed her to know him better, love him better, and had brought her out of isolation and towards good people. Each day her happiness grew and she tempered it around Ben because she worried it might be brash and sharp against his new, brilliant skin, but with Finn there wasn't anything she wouldn't do to show him the joy in the world, the joy in people.

CHAPTER 28

Grace turned away from the sink, gave April's shoulder a quick touch, and started gathering things: a book, a sweater, putting things into a small shoulder bag.

'What are you doing?' April asked.

'I'm going back to the hospital.'

'But they sent you home.'

'Someone needs to be there for Charlie.'

'They won't let …' April started but stopped as she saw her dad make an almost imperceptible movement, a plea.

'He's family and we have a right to be there. I don't know what I was thinking earlier when they persuaded me it was okay to leave. That boy needs to know he's not alone. To know that he's loved. We need to know it's okay to hope. That it's okay to love.'

Sonny filled the kettle again and took out travel mugs, dropping a tea bag into each. He tucked in his shirt and shifted himself more comfortably into his trousers, smoothed his almost absent hair. They both looked at Ben who was running around with Finn in the garden. He was finally tiring. Ben made a move with his body like a question and Grace waved them in. Ben swept him up and Finn curved into his shoulder, tiring, relaxed. They all looked at Ben, at the lie of his shoulders, the rate of his breath. How was he doing? How was he handling this?

Ben was crying and trying not to let Finn see it. April reached up and wiped his tears away. But they kept coming.

April started to look around for what she'd need for the walk home.

'You could all just stay here,' Grace offered.

April rubbed Grace's arm and kissed her cheek. 'Thanks, but I promised Finn he would be spending the night in my house in the woods. Plus, what's the point, none of you will be here.'

'But he'll be asleep soon.'

'It's not really about where he'll sleep, it's mostly about where he'll wake up.'

She gathered herself together, tying her jumper around her waist. She was still in her walking clothes.

Ben said, 'I'm coming with you.'

She nodded, a tired pleasure relaxing her shoulders. 'But Finn gets the bed.'

The siblings exchanged a quiet, sad smile. Ben could stay wherever he wanted, as long as he wanted. They'd never refuse each other anything, ever.

Ben pointed and she gathered a few of his things too.

There were bear hugs, longer than normal, firmer all around. Everyone was crying quietly but it didn't stop them from moving, from doing the things that needed to be done.

April kissed Sonny and Grace on the cheeks. Sonny gave her a short hug, while Grace's was longer. It was the same with Ben.

Perhaps the touches were more hesitant because they were more intimate and that was unfamiliar and forged right here on the spot.

I love you, Dad. I love you, Grace.

I love you, Patience. I love you, Ben.

They all kissed Finn, who was still in Ben's arms. He stirred and asked if his mum and dad and Star would be here soon for a good night kiss.

'You'll see them tomorrow,' Grace said.

And no one knew if she'd said the right thing.

'April,' Finn said. 'You carry me. You promised.'

April put him on her back and he put one hand on her shoulder and the other grasped her hair, gently, for balance, and the left through the backdoor. Ben walked beside them and they maintained a brisk pace. Finn had traveled this path a few times with April. Last time it was still light and he'd walked on ahead. Tonight, Finn fell asleep quickly and so she carried him, a cuckoo in her arms. They'd not quite been tricked into caring for him, but were not quite willing participants in this either, whatever this was or may become the next day or the day after that. They didn't know how to do this, and were woefully ill-equipped to raise a child. What they were to Finn would change. They would be something more intimate. Maybe together they'd learn how to let go of some grievances, how to hold onto other things, how to wear life more lightly.

April was thinking about how her aunt Grace used to nickname her girlfriends and nieces and nephew after flowers and warm seasons, and how they all went along with it, as if the renaming was a gift she gave to you, as if she saw the best there was in you, even if part of it was not yet true. It wasn't a lie because she believed it and you came to believe it too and it became something else closer to what the truth would be.

Finn murmured and pressed his lips and breath into April's neck but didn't wake until they were nearly at April's house. He squirmed, stretching his legs towards the ground and so April set him down, and Finn held Ben's hand, and April's too, and they stopped and listened to the sounds of the woods and took in the outlines of the trees and the flutter of the birds who were making the most of this lengthened day. He asked questions about some noises and other movements, which they answered as fully as they could.

April made some hot chocolate for each of them, lifted Finn and then sat him on her lap as he blew on it and took big sips, a generous splodge racing down the front of his shirt. He started to fall asleep again and she led him to her bed, took off his stained shirt, and he was tucked up and asleep in minutes. Sound asleep and worn out with his day.

They heard him from outside where they'd gone to sit: Finn laughed in his sleep. He'd always done that. Like Nic used to. He'll always do that. Arms moving like he was signing the funniest story or was the conductor not only of his dreams but of all dream worlds.

> *I don't think I ever did that.*
> *Me neither.*
> *It's amazing.*

CHAPTER 29

When Grace and Sonny returned to the hospital they found their way more easily to the ward. Grace had a small metal music box in her pocket. They sat in the nearly empty waiting room. A few people were stretched out over numerous chairs, with coats used as pillows, sleeves as tissues. Grace and Sonny sat side by side. Nothing was right in the world except that one of her oldest, most troublesome friends was beside her.

They leaned against each other at some point and found brief sleep. One or the other might wake and check in with Charlie's progress. It was nearly midnight when he was finally out of surgery.

He might not wake up, said the doctor, but you never know, something might get through.

They sat beside Charlie and it was Grace who told him he was not alone, and that his wife and daughter would be waiting for him. She kept it ambiguous. Thinking that if he recovered, he'd never remember her fib; if he died it was the right thing to know there would be people waiting for him.

*

With Finn asleep on April's bed, they'd opened the window so he could hear the woods, like he'd said he wanted. Ben sat on the log beside the fire April had lit. They were both drinking whisky, slowly, calmly.

Around them the forest was quiet but not quite completely dark as they all tipped over to the other side of the summer solstice. There was a barn owl out there quartering on some nights and a snipe too, calling out to define the sides of his territory, but tonight they were neither seen nor heard. April had a small clutch of wildflowers on the counter, two sets of car keys in her pocket, and a little boy asleep, thankfully, in her bed. It wouldn't get pitch dark tonight or any night this week. In some ways, whether they were aware of it or not, they all cast their gaze out on this the lightest and longest of days, as much as they'd spiral around its dark, short companion six months from now. It was a summer-lengthened twilight and she had such an urge to run to the top of the hill and walk amidst the ruins of an old clearance village, now surrendered to lichen and moss and new-growth forest.

The ruins were a collocation of stone houses and outbuildings, poked up through the grass and heather at the top of the hill and she and Nic used to run up from their aunt Grace's cottage, playing house, chasing imaginary hens and watching as a tiny fluttering birds sought shelter while a hawk circled overhead. Nic would try to order April around but April wouldn't have it; April tried to tell Nic what to do and she ignored her. They each set up their own households and did everything for themselves: the cooking, the cleaning, the chopping of wood. They drank beer like their dad and whisky like their aunt and told stories like their mum and smoked pipes like people on the telly, before running down the hill when called for dinner. There were miles they could see in each direction, not glimpsed through trees like now, but out over the open land of high moors. Where was Ben on these days? Swimming in the loch? Running wild with some boy he'd just met but who'd be his best friend within the hour? It didn't matter, for it was summer and they were there for each other if they were to shout.

Outside April's cottage, she and Ben, toasted Nic, Charlie and Star. They talked of leeches and the swing and how Nic's hands were always into everything, trying to figure out how things worked, and Ben's Sonia (fucking Sonia) and April's Col (lovely Col) and of giving into the urge to punch—how sweet it was, how satisfying, and how they both needed to stop giving in. They didn't know about Nic's time on Lewis, where she'd apprenticed with Donald, or other boyfriends or much of anything for those years, but they did know about swimming in lochs.

'Remember when she was about to have Finn?'

'It was way hotter than today and Nic was enormous.'

'And wearing a dress!'

And Ben told the story of his day that day, the epic journey he'd had and how worried he'd been about her, and how beautiful and awkward she'd looked.

'And I'll say it again. Huge.'

'We'll she was making that brilliant creature who is lying asleep in there.'

They stopped to listen to see if they were still able to hear him breathing or laughing through the open window, but couldn't.

'I'm falling over,' Ben said. 'We'll have long days ahead. I'm going to get some kip.'

'Take the bed,' April said. 'If Finn is hogging it, just shift him over.'

'You sure?'

'Yeah, I'm not ready to sleep and I might not be able to all night.'

He folded his arms around her and April realised she always thought of a hug with Ben as something that included Nic too. A strange noise between a gasp and a catch came from her chest and throat. Ben and April held each other, their bodies trying to assimilate knowledge and emotion they were not complex enough to handle. Eventually Ben pulled away and kissed April on the forehead. She nodded, 'I know, we can't stand here all night.'

'We could but you'd be holding me up.'

'I could do that.'

'Night, April.'

Her hands itched. She got her maul and gloves and took to splitting some wood.

Finn had been lying awake when Ben came in, but sleepily so, and when he got into bed Finn curled against him. 'Will you swim with me in the loch too?' Finn asked. Ah, the boy had been listening. 'Yes,' said Ben. 'We can do that anytime you like.' Ben laid awake feeling their chests rise and fall, listening to Finn breathe beside him; outside his sister's sure swing, her axe humming the air and cracking each log.

CHAPTER 30

Morning, After

April placed each log on the bigger stump she used as her chopping block. They were muckle things and even with her maul a few were damp and full of knots and she struggled to find the sweet spot that would crack each open. Often she got it first time and the two halves would burst out to the sides. Around her, neat, burnable logs were scattered. Tonight she had no interest in piling the wood, only in splitting it.

Her back ached and her legs were sore and stiff and finally she knew that this would not bring her sleep.

She texted Col. It was 4am.

You up?

Yes.

Fancy coming around?

You okay?

Nic's dead.

April, I'm so sorry.

Finn and Ben are here, sleeping.

On my way.

She'd never done anything like this before. Crying into a lover's chest without any filter. Steady, quiet sobbing.

Like her mother had done those last few years. It was embarrassing, when she looked back on it. But in the moment it had felt safe, like she could trust Col. They fell asleep on the sofa cushions laid out on the floor of the living room. Not something she'd want to do again anytime soon.

The hospital the day after Nic and Star died, the day Charlie died, was as you'd expect. No one was at their best. Grace and Sonny were with Charlie as he died. His parents arrived minutes too late, and none of the Avenses had changed a thing in the room since Charlie had stopped breathing. They stood to make room as soon as John and Siân arrived in the doorway but it made no difference. John was stoic, which in a single breath turned to fury. Rage at the Avenses. He waved his arms, stood between them and his son, gesturing for them to leave.

Siân went to the other side of the bed from her husband and paid him no heed. Her eyes were on Charlie. His hands in her hands, her lips to his cheek. In her there was only grief and only the sadness she would never shed of not being here for him before he died, as he died.

Grace invited them to her house later in the day, for some food, and company, she said, softly, and John refused. Saying only, 'We'll come by to pick Finn up. You will bring him out to the car.'

'He's not going anywhere.'

'John,' Siân said, looking to her husband, and then to her son, 'Charlie.' Nothing more. A father turned to his son. Grace thought she saw a ripple down the muscles in his back, his T-shirt in the breeze, a few hairs blew across Charlie's forehead too, from the open window, which Siân then closed. Too much like life in the room, Grace thought, and agreed with the action. Charlie's mother pulled the blinds closed and the room cooled, became a place of mourning.

That night at Grace's they waited for a car to pull up. April had wanted to take Finn into the woods, hiding him away like a fugitive. Grace had said she needed to use her head more. 'We can't be the antagonists here. Where are they going to keep him? In a tiny B&B room. No, he stays here. We will not be held hostage by a man in a rage.'

'Although I could see you giving into her,' Ben said. 'Siân

wouldn't say anything but just take Finn's hand and lead him away. And we'd let her go.'

'She won't. She is taking time to grieve her son. She's not ready to take care of the living yet.'

Despite Grace's firm views, over the next few days, the rest of the family found ways to keep Finn away from Grace's. Sonny finding outings to take Finn on, always leaving quite early in the morning. Simply not being at home, evading the Skirvings. So Charlie's parents, who had stopped by Grace's a few times only to find it empty or empty of Finn, were mad, as things went, when it came to the funeral, custody of Finn and the croft.

April and Col were up early and sitting on the couch with coffee when Finn came in and sat beside Col. Ben followed and clattered around the kitchen.

'Who are you?' asked Finn.

'I'm Col.'

'Col,' Finn repeated, peering. His brows arching. 'Are you a boy or a girl?'

Col didn't flinch and didn't look at April or Ben. 'Both,' Col said, looking at Finn directly. This was clearly not the first time Col had fielded this question from a child. Ben looked to April and back to Col, and shook his head as pieces fell into place.

'How?' Finn asked.

April was interested in the answer too. She was still learning what it meant for Col, in Col's own words.

'We're all both in here,' Col said pointing at a breastbone. 'Sometimes we feel we're a bit more of one or the other. For me it's equal and I'm the same on the outside. Sometimes you can feel one way on the inside but feel like you have to be another on the outside. And that can be hard. For me, what's on the inside is on the outside.'

Finn sat between them and looked up at Col. He did not ask any more questions but he was fascinated. He took Col's hand.

'Will you come for a walk with us? Uncle Ben said we'll walk back to great-aunt Grace's.'

'I'd love to. I'll come part of the way but then I need to go to work.'

April didn't know if that was still true or if it was a way for Col to leave the family alone with the day.

She couldn't decipher the look on Ben's face. It was cheeky but also edgier.

'A four-year-old clocked it in a minute,' he said shaking

his head. 'How does that work, between you?' Ben asked. You could tell he wanted to ask Col what bits Col had and Ben was looking and trying to figure it out.

'None of your business,' April said.

'Aren't you a charmer, first thing in the morning,' said Col to Ben.

'I don't know what you are.'

'I'm the same as you.' Col said it in an even voice and met Ben's gaze. It wasn't an accusation. It wasn't tit for tat. 'We wear it differently, but you and me, this everything all at once, with our differences that we're born with and how we also choose to wear them, and what the outside world thinks of us. And how we both say no, not this, but yes, this. We're the same.'

Ben drank his coffee and Finn, who still had a hold of Col's hand, slid off the couch pulling Col to standing. 'Let's go to Aunt Grace's. I want to see Mum and Dad and Star.'

And there it was. What today was about.

Col walked to the top of the hill with them, since they'd taken the long way via the ruins, which gave them more time to try to figure out what to say to Finn.

'Good luck today. Take time for yourselves. Don't let the practicalities define what these days are. It's too easy to do.' April and Col kissed and she wanted to bend into it, be held and taken care of but they simply kissed and Col headed back down.

As they walked, a story April had been thinking about writing came to her; one she somehow wanted to make into a song. She didn't know how to do it yet, but the story came to her now and she asked Finn if he'd like to hear it.

'What kind of story is it?'

'A kind story.'

'One that feels like this?' Finn said and he made a movement of one hand to his heart like Ben did, like grandpa did. Ben had to look away to see himself so clearly in this child and that this gesture of sadness looked like one of hope to his nephew. 'Yes, like that,' April said, gently rubbing Ben's shoulder and back, waiting for the hard breaths to pass, to ease into the walking again.

On a little croft, in the far north.

'The one I live on. That one?'

'Yes, there. *Lived a dancing family.*'

'Is that all they did, dance?'

'No, but when they greeted each other they'd shake their booties, they'd open their arms and skirl.

The Birlin' Skirvings, that's what they were called. And sometimes they danced just the four of them in greeting, in celebration, in sadness and in joy, and at other times their family from the south would travel north to join them and they were the Happening Avenses and Hopping Aunt Hallan dancing with the Birling Skirvings and other people, friends and neighbours and strangers from far and wide would come and watch them all dance, and sometimes these others would join them, and the whole croft would be alive with people dancing and laughing.

'And singing!' Finn said.

'Yes,' April said. 'And how were they singing?'

'Out of tune.'

'Because it was the most beautiful sound in the world,' Ben added. 'What might that sound like?'

Finn howled like a wolf and April and Ben joined him.

'But some of them sang in tune too, but quietly, trying not to draw attention to themselves, but their voices were clear and rang out.'

And the three of them tried to sing like the wren, which is small but has a big song.

April imagined herself sitting on a plain wooden chair with her mandolin, in the corner of the pub with the noise and the conversation happening all around her and she'd sing this song she'd not yet written, and she'd take up just enough space and some people would turn in her direction and listen and the air in the room would change, the song would make space for everyone. Some would continue their conversations, but softer with laughter and small touches on an arm, and maybe, she'd like to think, they'd sing parts of her song to themselves later, because even as they talked, they heard her.

'And when they danced the days were woven in light and when they rested their voices could be heard in the dark.

'Sometimes when one of them had to go away and the others wanted to see them again even if they were far away, they'd know they were there dancing in the wind that blew the snow into eddies or when the sun rose with pinks and oranges and reds, and they heard them again in the settling of the house and the calling of the stags. And if they were ever thinking they were forgetting anything about those who were far away, they asked all the people who love them, and they'd help call them to this place, for the dance was known by all the people who knew them and watched them and loved them.'

Finn knew this dance and let go and stomped and turned and whooped—he left space for his mum and dad, who had Star bound to his chest, and in the summer morning there was so much brightness it made April and Ben's eyes hurt and let loose the tears that had gathered there.

CHAPTER 31

One day tipped over into yet another and through this strange solstice light, April and Col slow-danced around the house and out into the garden and beyond into the woods, smelling the pine resin on her hands from splitting wood and the sweet edge of garlic on Col's, left over from making dinner, and they tasted salt as lips met a neck.

In the morning they'd pick up Grace and Sonny and all travel north to Ben's house, which had been their sister's house, where the whole family would gather, as they did each year on this day.

They'd pass the place of the accident, as Ben, Siân and Finn did nearly every day. Sometimes someone said something; sometimes they didn't, and often one of them started singing, off key, on purpose. Or told a story of way back when, just because. Other people who were not Finn's family didn't mention it when they drove by and they turned the radio up or asked him a question about his day.

Finn couldn't know what happened. No one could. You might conjecture, which was the word April used. Grace said,

Imagine. Grandma Siân said it was a mystery. Ben's hand danced towards his heart, *Hey little fellow, I wouldn't worry about it.*

Finn imagined his mum and how she laughed and how it filled up the space of the car. She'd gather them all into her joy. First Star and then his dad. On this day, she'd have turned to look at them, sometimes Dad sat in back without a seatbelt, which Mum scolded him for, and he'd entertain Star, if she was tetchy. His mum, because that's the sort of day it was, threw her head back and her arms open, just for a second, one arm stretching beyond the open window, open on the June day. Star had bright red cheeks, glistening from the unexpected heat of the day and her recent feed. His mum always fed Star before a car journey. His dad laughed too, deep and it had a red to it, of lips and gums and love, like a valentine's red heart. This much Finn knew, even as he imagined. He conjectured that his dad laughed as the car settled into the trip to Achiltibuie where they'd collect Finn. Then his dad said, *Nic. Nic!*

Finn thought about it. There must have been a deer or a hare or even a pheasant. Something that made her swerve. That's what people said. He thought, imagined, conjectured, and did not worry.

Even now he did not worry. It didn't change anything, Grace said, and he knew it was true. All he remembered of his parents and of Star was love and that seemed to have got him through okay so far.

There were orange cones there for a while. When April and his grandad had picked him up that day, when they drove past, they were singing one of his favourite songs and none of them stopped singing, but they both grew quieter and looked out the window and so did he and saw the fresh car tracks cutting a muddy, rocky path through the heather.

This was a family that kept their eyes on the promise of the future while they lived the everyday knowledge of the past. By living it they believed they would all know the best of it.

Finn knew it too and thought of what he knew as brilliantly bright, impossibly gathered. It was what made joy possible. For years he'd been watching his family. Specifically, he watched each individual who made up his family. Some were linked to him by blood, but others had been acquired over time. He was someone who didn't worry or fuss overly. Some people thought it was because of everything that happened, that it was a stoic quiet, but he knew it was just the way he was, the way he would have been anyway.

He'd always been a quiet kid and he was now becoming a quiet man. He was quiet, except when he laughed, which he did often, or when he danced, which he did well and exuberantly, and he'd be the one to invite the taciturn person onto the floor for a Gay Gordons, the person tapping their foot but burdened with a lead-footed date who wouldn't dance. He told stories about this person or that, sometimes out loud, sometimes in his head, and they were often stories he'd heard or witnessed or embellished or conjectured that he then told and retold to himself. He carried them as songs too, as music, as breath and heartbeat. It sounded romantic but wasn't. It's what we all do. How we tell these stories alters how we meet the future. Sometimes it was Grandpa Sonny or April or Ben or Grace or Grandma Siân he'd pulled onto the dance floor or into song.

And over the years, on the way home from a ceilidh at the community hall or dinner at a pub or traveling back from Grace's, the adults had told stories to each other. He used to think they thought he was asleep, but now he knew they'd always hoped he was awake for it all.

ACKNOWLEDGEMENTS

Thank you to my eclectic, made and chosen family, you have all been here as I consider how we may hold, support and remember those who are dear to us. Thank you to ARTT—it is a joy to spend life with you. A special thanks to Jean who has been here for me, for us, with wit, gardening and word-games through the years. I started this book at the practical and magical MacDowell Colony, and the place and the brilliant collocation of people gathered there that spring is in here too. Thank you to Tom, Rosie and Kate at Penned in the Margins—it has been a fantastic process and I appreciate the care and enthusiasm you give to this and all your books. A resounding and grounding thank you to Laura Macdougall, the best agent a writer could ask for. The Scottish Highlands are everywhere in this book, and the time I've spent here has been the making of so much of how I understand and write about this world—as it is, as it may become.